NOW SHOWING

Mondo Apocalypto!

An Ascendent Publishing Title
All Rights Reserved® Winter 2022 Issue #1

Staff/Contributing Writers:

Chris Philbrook
Melody Alice
Misha Tuesday
Shannon Humphreys
Harmony Balizet
Nick Holland

Staff/Contributing Artists:

Michael Strong
Nix Black
Lilith Celeste

Associate Editor: Lucienne LeBeau

Managing Editor: w.p. Quigley

DOUBLE FEATURE

First:
A Word From Our Projectionist...

Hi there! Welcome to the first issue, book, collection, or whatever the hell you want to call it of "DOUBLE FEATURE". This whole thing was my ridiculous idea, so if you're looking for someone to blame/hold responsible, it's me.

Name's Wally, but when I write I go under the pen name of w.p. Quigley — an homage to one of my influences, the mostly misunderstood, misinterpreted, shut-in, and legendary weirdo, H.P. Lovecraft. The lowercase thing with the initials shows up from time to time.

Each issue will kick off with a "projectionist" doing an introduction and synopsis of the two "films" (short novellas) for the 'ish, as well as some stuff about the "directors" (authors). There'll be an 'Intermission' as well, which for now will be a wild card as to what that will entail from issue to issue. I decided to drop a little history of that most essential staple of any moviegoing experience — popcorn. Why the fuck do we all eat popcorn at the movies anyway? I ask the hard questions at 'intermission', for you, dear reader.

Couple of "Short FIlms" to get us started though. There's "Amanda" from Melody Alice, and "Tomorrow" from Chris Philbrook. They're handling warm-up duties just this first issue, but in the coming year they'll be in that spotlight - after you read their offerings, I'm sure you won't be able to wait to read what they do next.

So welcome to the show...just a couple of things before we begin, though. Disclaimers, waivers, ipso factos and such.

We have...intentions here in the DOUBLE FEATURE management offices. Nothing nefarious, of course. Kind of altruistic, actually.

Okay, maybe some nefarious intentions. But the good kind of nefarious. Whatever.

The first is to provide a platform for new and upcoming authors to showcase and/or publish their work – without having to surmount the prohibitive and daunting task of finishing an entire book. Each of our issues will be clocking in at about a hundred manuscript pages, which is twenty-five thousand words if you're scoring at home.

A writer doesn't really start talking about being able to kick out a 'book' until they've got something that's twice that in length, and that's a tough hurdle to get over. It was the biggest hurdle for me, anyway - actually fucking finishing something long enough to publish. This represented such a frustratingly difficult milestone to hit that it ended up taking me twenty years of false starts, half-finished ideas, attention deficit disorder distractions, and just general life nonsense to reach it. I finally pulled it off twice this year, a novel and an anthology. The anthology is out, the novel drops next year. It's a struggle, it sucks, but once you're over it you're over it and it makes moving forward WAY easier to do.

I figure I'd make it easier for those out there who possess the same attention-based impediment as yours truly to get something out there, and DOUBLE FEATURE is here for it. In reading our horrid little publication, you'll be supporting them as well. Good on ya', sport.

The second intention is to present DOUBLE FEATURE as a loving homage and tribute to those magical nights at drive-in movie theatres and grindhouses across this "great" land of ours. Drive-Ins were some of the few entities in the past few years to have benefitted from the worldwide outbreak of COVID-19, as packing a room with people sitting inches and feet apart was a non-starter for traditional theatres to continue business as usual.

Holy shit.
He's Still Going, Isn't he?

I fucking love drive-in theatres, despite the fact the you can always count on the picture quality to suck monster cock, as well as no less than ten to fifteen absolute fucking dunces who leave their headlights on, compulsively shout dumbass, obvious jokes the entire night, or change their spot eleven times because their date can't see the screen.

Don't forget that Chinese Water Torture that awaits at the end of the evening either – the convoy of cars and the endless wait to get out of the drive-in once the movies are done. Mmmm...that's good aggravation. But the movies they'd show at those outdoor temples to cheeseball entertainment? Solid fucking gold. Last one I went to had a double billing of "Evil Dead" and "I sadly am too young to have ever experienced a true grindhouse theatre. I'm sure I'd find shit to bitch about those, too. I'd still love the hell out of them. There's something uniquely American about these establishments, and it's the kind of American institution that transcends political, social, or religious affiliations. Drive-in theatres and grindhouses possess some kind of supernatural yet (un) wholesome power to bring purveyors of beautiful trash together - and they've proved to be one of the few things that still do despite the waking nightmare our nation and culture have devolved into. We celebrate our love of the stories and films that the rest of "normative" society discards and dismisses.

The third reason is that the idea is...well... it's just fucking cool. No more need be said about that.

Admission is dirt fucking cheap too, and always will be at DOUBLE FEATURE. And those bucks you drop on an issue pays for the next one after that. This'll be our DOUBLE FEATURE guarantee to you, our beloved supporters.

Comfy? Cool.

This theatre has no name, other than the one you assign it. We may pick the films, but we're here in the mind of every reader that opens the cover and takes in the stories that are within.

You, dear reader, can call it whatever you want - but make sure it's cool. Use scary and badass words, vaguely threatening and inviting at the same time.

The two tales inside our inaugural issue (or "night" if we're really stretching the metaphor) are a couple of piping hot 'n' fresh ones from my demonstrably damaged imagination. The first was inspired by a social media meme I saw one September night. The second came from a passing comment made by an old friend while kayaking down a river in Pembroke, Massachusetts.

Neither story ended up bearing any resemblance to the original idea.

These "movies" in addition to the two "short films" make up what I'm calling "Mondo Apocalypto!" and follow the word 'apocalypse' as a central theme, but in a different sense of the word in each narrative.

My writing is driven by an undercurrent of self and sanity preservation, a kind of solo therapy session. The actual horror I see, experience, and infer almost daily builds up, then gets kicked back onto a page or thirty — and I get to go on pretending like I'm good with how fucked the world is.

These "movies" are really ways for me to cope with the rapid de-evolution and disintegration of mankind's higher functionalities via mass media and technology. I can't speak for Melody or Chris though. They'd probably just smile and nod and mouth the words "just go along with him".

They're fun though. I promise.
Alright, I'm done.
Let's start the fucking show.

-WP Quigley
Head Fucknut

5

TONIGHT'S DIRECTORS:

Featured Director: W . P . Q u i g l e y
"Gary Spivey (Has Foreseen This" & "DVD Extras"

Melody Alice - "A m a n d a"

Chris Philbrook - "Tomorrow"

Contributing Artist: M i c h a e l   S t r o n g

Creative/Art Director: N i x   B l a c k

Short Films

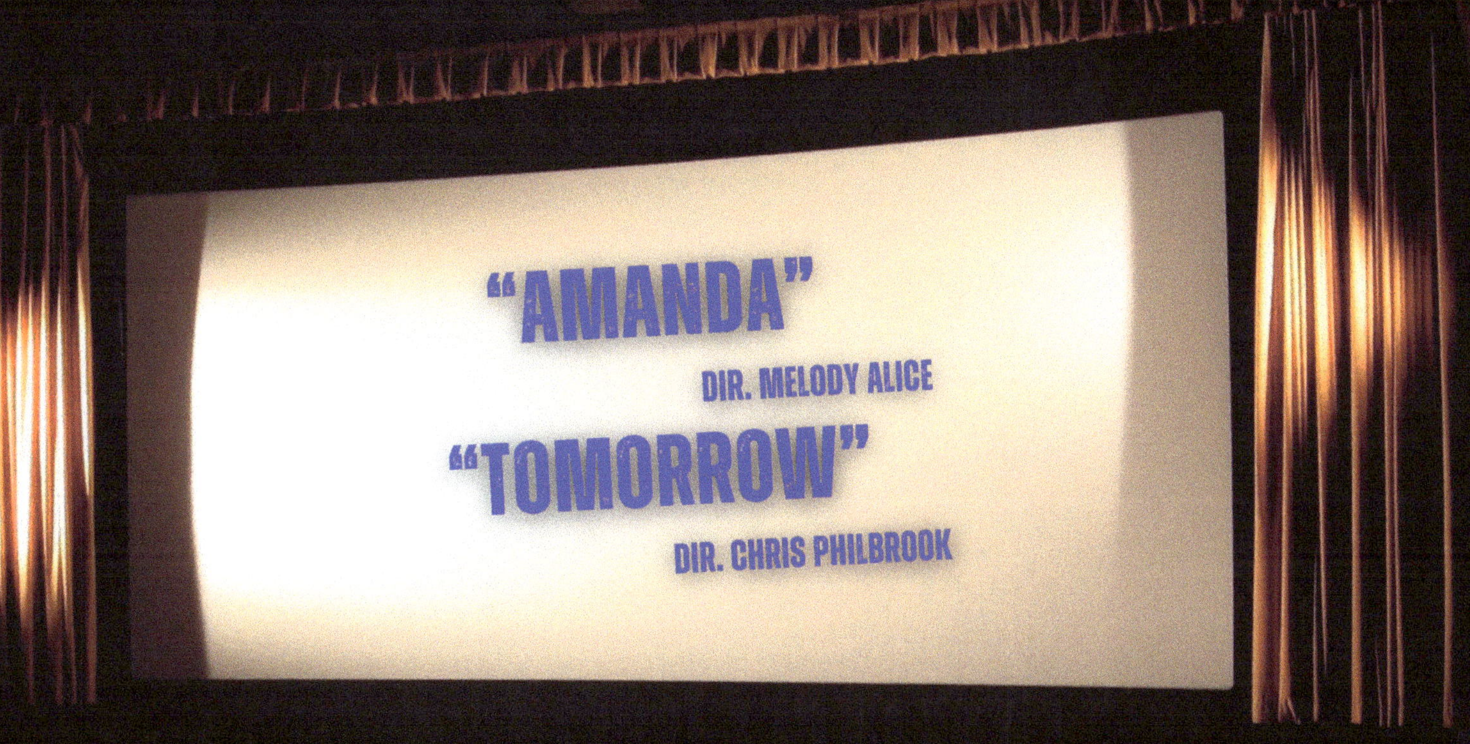

AMANDA:

A romantic rendezvous
Two lovers: Life...and Death
Will one see the forest for the trees?

TOMORROW:

No more teachers, no more books
No more innocent flirtatious looks
When the machine rings that bell
Time will only tell . . .

"A m a n d a"
M e l o d y   A l i c e

She watched him flip another page of the book he was reading with his thumb.

'How did he do that so smoothly?' she wondered.

His posture always was so relaxed, coffee cup steaming in his other hand whenever he made that deft maneuver. A lock of hair fell in front of his eyes - but just a brief flash of annoyance as he placed the cup down on the log in front of him to tuck the lock back behind his ear.
He was reading his much-loved copy of Conrad's *Heart of Darkness* again, the spine creased so badly to be unrecognizable as such. But she knew him so well. Of course he was reading it again. She'd even sat through the movie version, *Apocalypse Now,* on one of their date nights. One of the few that they'd spent at his apartment before finding this, their special place.

She loved those secret meetings between them in the forest; no noise from the city, and away from any too-curious looks from her peers on campus. Here, he wasn't her professor, and she wasn't his student. There were no lectures. Just quiet companionship, accompanied only by the sounds of an occasional wind through the leaves or birdsong.

It was still today, though, and dark - except for the light from his small camping lantern it would have been pitch this far into the woods. They had never come here at night before. He'd said before that he liked to be able to see her when they made love beneath the trees.

How had she not noticed the day slipping away? Had she dozed in the afterglow longer than she had thought? Her spot under the old oak was so cozy - its roots made almost perfect armrests and the ground was always shaded and cool. She loved the scent of the dirt and moss beneath her. This had always been her spot, however, and thus couldn't possibly held be responsible for her loss of time.
She turned her attention back to her lover. He hadn't looked over at her once since. Their companionship was usually more intimate. It was endearing how engrossed he became when something took hold of his interest.

Or someone, she thought impishly, thinking of how the attraction between them had grown over the semester. At least until he had brought her to this beautiful and secret spot that became the site of their ritual.

His hair escaped again and this time, he left it where it fell across his vision. She noticed for the first time the grey that streaked through that meddlesome lock of hair. Was it a trick of the lantern light in the dark perhaps? He was the youngest Ethics professor that the University had ever hired. Surely too young to already have a streak the full length of his hair, reaching all the way to his chin? She found that she rather liked it, this new, distinguished element.
Seeing that streak of grey made her wonder what else about him she might have missed. For all the time she spent gazing at him, it was inconceivable that she could have overlooked this change. Wait, there was something else.

Lines around his eyes. Crow's feet? Still handsome, but why did he suddenly look so. . . old?

She was still so tired..but hadn't she just woken from a nap? She bore down with her thoughts and concentrated. This sharpened her vision. It had been to see clearly in the dark and from her angle on the ground. But there was more. She hadn't noticed the extra weight around his waist, obscured by his puffy jacket.

Still so hard to focus. Her senses that wanted to be full only of him were instead hyper-aware of the scents and texture all around her.

The damp, cool earth.

The hard feel of the roots underneath her.

The soil brimming full of life all around her..and yet, silent. Insects sleeping peacefully until spring. Plants dormant all around her, through her.

Alarm suddenly seized her.

The stillness was broken, as a wind blew through the trees, ruffling the pages of his book until finally he looked to her, in the direction the sudden gust had come from.

"That you, sweet Lizzy?" he grinned, before draining the last of his coffee and returning to his book.

Her name wasn't Lizzy. Or Elizabeth. Not even fucking close.

He doesn't even remember which of us is buried where.

The thought wasn't hers. It came from close to her, from the ground nearby. No, from the ground within her. They were all connected, here inside the earth.

With a rush, she remembered the hammer coming down. How long had she been here, buried beneath the tree they had made love under?

She tried, to feel her body around her but there was nothing. She knew then that she had been the first. He hadn't honed his method yet. He'd buried her too shallowly, but luck had been with him. She was deep enough in the woods that the animals that dug her up had done the work of hiding her body for him. Some consuming what they could at the spot, others carrying her in pieces back to their dens. But still some of her had seeped and soaked into this ground, feeding the soil and remaining here with the rest that would join her over the years.
She tried to extend her consciousness as it still remained, as far as it would go. She couldn't tell how many others there were. She caught fragments of their memories as surely as they must have been caught fragments of hers. Their collective pain and despair transferred between them as fluidly as the nutrients from their bodies had done with the earth that now held them all.

The others had all been around her age. Sex workers from the city. Store clerks and fast food workers that had the misfortune of closing up for the night alone. Here in the soil, they were all the same.

Girls, some just barely women, whose lives had been cut short by this man. This man that came here and sat calmly reading Joseph Conrad while surrounded by his victims. This man was the apocalypse.

The scent of the ground around her intensified, their collective rage bubbling beneath the surface. They could all see him quite clearly now, despite the darkness. They knew themselves, and they knew him, finally, for what he was. They were awake. . .

. . .and they weren't alone anymore.

They had each other. Sisters by cruel fate, but sisters nonetheless.

He didn't notice as the earth turned muddy beneath him, slowly packing itself into the ridges of his hiking boots. It wasn't until the log he was sitting on began to sink, tipping him sideways and on to the ground that he finally realized that something was wrong.

The book sank almost immediately. As he reached for it in confusion, he realized that he couldn't turn, in any direction, to retrieve his balance. He was stuck in the rapidly softening ground. He reached for a nearby root to try to pull himself up, but it broke off.

As he looked at the useless piece of root in growing frustration, he saw that it wasn't a detached root at all... and let out his first scream.

He threw the rotted remains of a leg to the side and tried to gather his wits. He was brilliant after all. Whatever was happening had an explanation and there had to be a way out. He just had to stay calm. On his back and still slowly sinking with soil filling his ears, he tried to regulate his breathing to make another attempt to lift himself up. That was when he felt his body cradled by that of his most recent victim.

Now sans the leg that had been thrown aside, she lay the full length beneath him, the back of his skull against her soft, decaying flesh. As he tried to lift his head, there was a sickening, sucking sound as parts of her flesh came away and stuck in his hair. In a full panic now, he reached down to steady himself. He'd use the bitch to gain his balance, sit up, and get out of here. This was a mistake.

His hand met with no resistance at all, as it sank deep into her exploded, distended abdominal cavity and became tangled in the coiled mush of her intestines. Now past being able to hold back his screams, his head involuntarily jerked back in his panic.

With an audible crack, his head slammed through her ribs and was now nestled inside her chest cavity.

As the nearby ground and soil continued to swallow him, teeming with death instead of life as it consumed, he became faintly aware of the sounds of bodies sliding their way towards him... in all of their varied states of deterioration. Breaking up and coming together to form a liquid, writhing pool beneath him.

Finally, as a trickle of foetid earth worked its way up and into his nose, he heard a voice that he had long forgotten. The one that had started it all for him. He grimaced as the swampy rivulets sank between his lips, coating his teeth and forcing itself down his throat.

"Amanda?" he choked out with the last of his breath before the earth completely filled him, having now successfully breached all of his soft open parts.

Now you remember me, she thought, and the thought was whispered on the soft breath of wind through the trees, but he was now past hearing.

A cool breeze blew through the cafeteria of the high school. Girls huddled together under their puffy jackets, and the boys acted tough in their t-shirts. A thousand meaningless conversations kept almost all of them on pins and needles as they each tried to define who they were, and what they were going to be in this place, and in what life waited beyond.

"I'm so glad I won't have to worry anymore," Aleks said to his best friend Courtland. "One and done."

"It was painless man," Courtland said. "You just sit down, and the machine turns on, and you can read a book or whatever." Courtland chewed and swallowed a mouthful of flavorless cafeteria "chicken" nugget. "Tell me how it goes in the morning."

"Can't use your phone though," Aleks replied, as if he'd heard none of what Courtland had just said. Several of the puff-wrapped girls walked by, and the two teenagers halted their conversation to eyeball them.

Mostly they watched their hips.
The boys sighed.

"The machine will fry it," Courtland said. "And then? No more digging scandalous pictures on PixaTron for you."

"PixaTron is for losers, like you," Aleks said with a grin. "Not me though, bro. I'm a renaissance man. I've been joining old forum sites. No pictures allowed, no personal details allowed. Totally under the radar. You just talk about stuff that's interesting. I just joined one that's all about 4x4 off roading. Pretty cool."

"You're never going to afford a car," Courtland said.

"And you're never gonna get a girlfriend."

The girls departing giggled at the cafeteria's armed sentry as they left. The man in the black uniform paid them no attention, and kept his weapon aimed at the floor.

The bus ride home dragged on for about thirteen hours, Aleks reckoned. He passed the time listening to music on his ear buds, and did his best to ignore the few kids whose families were cleared for neural implants. They could listen to their music directly streamed into their senses without any kind of device. The real high end implants could even overlay video right on top of your regular vision. None of the kids with those implants rode buses, though.

No sense being envious. The right people got the right things, after all. The bus slowed, and came to a creaking stop.

"Perham Street," the guard at the front cage of the bus called out.

Aleks stood from his aged vinyl seat and slung his clear backpack over his shoulder. He turned sideways and shuffled down the center of the bus, trying hard to not bump into the kids sitting against the aisle. He failed several times, smacking several of his fellow teens on the shoulder, or the back of the head.

"Sorry. I'm sorry," he said each time. They accepted his apologies, or ignored him, as appropriate.

The guard threw the latch holding the gate shut then stepped into the open space behind the driver so the door could open. Always surly, the guard stared at Aleks until the kid skipped down the stairs to freedom. Aleks didn't look back, and started walking down the street to the multifamily house his parents rented a portion of. No one walked by him, and the only car that that passed was an armored government security tank. The man standing in the hatch on the top didn't swivel the gun towards Aleks—unlike the gunner two days ago—and it almost looked like he was going to wave.

He didn't. That'd be a breach of professional ethics, surely. After the heavy-wheeled vehicle rumbled by, Aleks crossed the street through its acrid exhaust plume. He passed the abandoned home that smelled like urine—holding his breath the whole time—and let himself in the back door of his home using the solitary key he had.

Yes, some families still used keys, though Aleks wasn't sure why. No one wanted to steal anymore. He walked in. His mom sat at the cluttered kitchen table on a worn wooden chair that didn't match, that tipped side to side with a clunk when you shifted your weight.

"Oh, hey," his mother said, wiping her eyes with a tissue. "You're home. I lost track of time. I'm sorry."

"Were you crying?" he asked her. "Everything okay?"

"Oh, no. Just some allergies. Pollen, I think. We had a few allergy pills left in the closet and I took one. I'm feeling much better."

Aleks didn't believe her, but he didn't press.

"Ready to go?" she asked him, standing up from her seat at the table.

"Yeah, I've been ready all day. Is Dad coming?"

"No, honey. He uh, he had to stay at the facility longer tonight. Quotas, or something," she said with a wince.

Aleks didn't believe her, but he didn't press. His was a skilled worker. They often made him stay late.

Aleks went to the bathroom then grabbed a piece of

bread with butter on it to eat. The mother gathered her

few things, and they departed the house together.

Arm in arm they walked down the same empty street, past the same stench-ridden corpse of a home, all the way to the same bus stop Aleks got off at earlier. The air was crisp, the sun shined, and for a boy, this was good.

Another gun truck rolled by before the bus and all four of its passengers came, and after they were let through the inner gate and took their seats, it took off.

Aleks was excited, but he wasn't so sure about his mom.

"Let me help you," he said to her as they disembarked.

"Hurry up," the bus guard urged. "We're on a schedule."

"I'm sorry," she said, stepping down the stairs with a stiff back. "These bus rides are murder on my back."

"It won't matter much longer, so hurry up," the guard said, disgusted.

"Sorry," Aleks said, helping his mother down and out.

The accordion door of the city transport slammed shut behind her, nearly clamping down on the end of her scarf. She recoiled away as the driver gunned the motor, pulling them back onto the empty streets, and towards their next stop. They turned, and looked at their destination.

The building was forgettable in every way, save for how clean the outside was, and how bright the bricks on its side were. Two of the wheeled military vehicles sat in a delta pattern near the steel front door and a dozen of the black-uniformed, armed soldiers stood all about. No signs adorned the building, and two nondescript sedans parked off to the side indicated that few people worked here.

Aleks contained the urge to run, or at least bounce his way to the door. The mother and son walked arm in arm between the cordon of guards, and to the metal door. Aleks pulled the handle, and it stayed put.

"Scan your arm," one of the guards said. It sounded rehearsed.

"Oh yeah, sorry," he said.

Aleks pulled his left sleeve up, revealing his citizen identification bar code. He held it under a small metal box that hung near the door, and a red laser scanned it. A moment after, a mechanical click sounded behind the wall. He pulled the handle again, and the door opened. He walked in, trailing his mother. Her allergies were acting up again.

After walking down a white hallway, with white lights, they entered a white room. A steel door with no knows or handles was embedded in the far wall. To the right there was one gurney covered in white sheets. On those sheets were blue nurse's scrubs folded sharp enough to cut. Beside the bed was a metal tray, and on that tray there was a small plastic bottle.

Three sentences were stenciled in red onto the wall above the bed:

PUT ON THE SCRUBS

DRINK THE CONTENTS OF THE BOTTLE

SIT ON THE BED – SOMEONE WILL BE WITH YOU SHORTLY

Aleks got to work. He didn't pause until all that remained was his underwear. He turned and looked back at his mom, who had put her face in the opposite corner of the room.

"Should I take my underwear off?"

"Probably," she answered. Her tiny voice echoed out of the corner walls, doubling itself, but somehow sounding smaller.

Aleks pulled his stained boxers off and tossed them on the bed. He pulled the blue trousers on, then slid his meager torso into the blue shirt. He hopped up onto the bed and let his legs dangle.

"You're ready?" his mother asked, still looking away.

"Yup," Aleks said. "Super ready."

"I'm going to step outside. I need a cigarette," she said. "I'll be waiting for you out there."

"Okay, love you."

"Love you too," she said, and left down the hall.

Aleks heard the outer door open, then snap shut.

He picked up the bottle and read the small label on the side. A barcode matching the one on his arm was center, and the number the government had assigned him was below it. He unscrewed the cap, and swallowed the whole bottle in six chugs.
It had the flavor of nuts, but a metallic aftertaste.

"Not bad," he said. He screwed the cap back on, and returned it to the tray.

Then, it was him, and the waiting.

The Processor came in through the embedded door. It slid sideways into the wall and he came in with purpose. His chin set, his face smiling, he came right over to Aleks and presented a hand scanner.

"Hi, I'm Aleks."

The scanner beeped, and the man read the display on the other side.

"I see that. Nice to meet you. We don't give names out here. Keeps it more... clinical," he explained.

"Makes sense," the teen said, but it didn't, not really.

"We're going to wheel you into the next room and get you in the machine. Takes about an hour, start to finish, and there are books you can read."

"It doesn't hurt, right?"

The man laughed. "You kids are always afraid we're going to hurt you. Why would we want to hurt you? We want this process to be easy. Not scary."

"How many more need it?"

"I wouldn't know," he explained as he sat the scanner down and wheeled Aleks through the doorway. "Not as many as before, but still quite a few. We're only ten years into the program."

"Is it weird to feel relief?" Aleks asked as the nurse, or doctor, or whatever he was pushed him across the next white room to a machine that looked like a giant rim with a dentist's chair sat in the middle. Aleks hadn't been to the dentist in years. Only the right people got that kind of care.

"You should feel relieved. You're helping to address a major issue facing our great society, as well as being quite the responsible adult. Plus, as you're already likely aware, I can then certify your code, and you're free to start dating."

" I can't wait, I've been..."

"Hop off," he said. " And Have a seat."

The nurse/doctor/soldier didn't care about what his immediate dating plans might have entailed.

Aleks did so.
The seat contoured to him.
The man hit some switches and the seat reclined a bit, and straightened his pelvis out, presenting his groin. A giant arm, not unlike the lights the dentist used to peer into his mouth swung around then, and the processor aimed the end of it directly at that spot. It looked like a donut, just like the donut that stood on end around him.

"Any specific book you want?"

"Are we ready?" Aleks asked.

"Yeah, this is it. The machine pops on, you'll hear some buzzing, some slight vibrations, and a faint tingle all over. About 45 minutes of that, we toggle it off, run our evaluation, and if it went well, I laser your code addendum onto your arm and you're free to go."

"That part hurts, right?"

"Yeah it's like a tattoo, but you're a tough guy. Your kind are tough," he said, patting him on the head. "Want to read the book about why?"

"Um, you don't have any comics?"

"Nah. The last guy ran off with the few we had left. Should've expected it, considering."

"Okay, I'll take it," Aleks said. It didn't matter anyway, he couldn't stop grinning.

Tomorrow... he could start dating.
He could start being a man.

The Processor went to a distant desk across the room and retrieved a small book. He returned, and handed it to Aleks.

The teenager leaned his head back, took a deep breath, and addressed the book in his hands. He skipped the first chapter, the introduction, and went straight to the second:

CHAPTER 2:

WHY MUST MY PEOPLE BE STERILIZED?

A STUDY IN ELIMINATING GENETIC DEAD ENDS FOR THE BETTERMENT OF EARTH
AND FOR PREVENTION OF GLOBAL CATASTROPHE AND APOCALYPSE

The machine hummed on, and just like the processor said, it tingled.

Aleks grinned. Tomorrow, he could start dating. He could start living. Even if it meant that today, part of him had to die.

Tomorrow.

This has been "Tomorrow" by contributing writer Chris Philbrook.

Chris is the USA TODAY bestselling author of the Diggory Finch, Ghosts, and Undead Diary series.

www.thechrisphilbrook.com

And more in the theme of...

MASCULINITY: TOXIC

Double Feature
7:30 pm (Presentation 1):

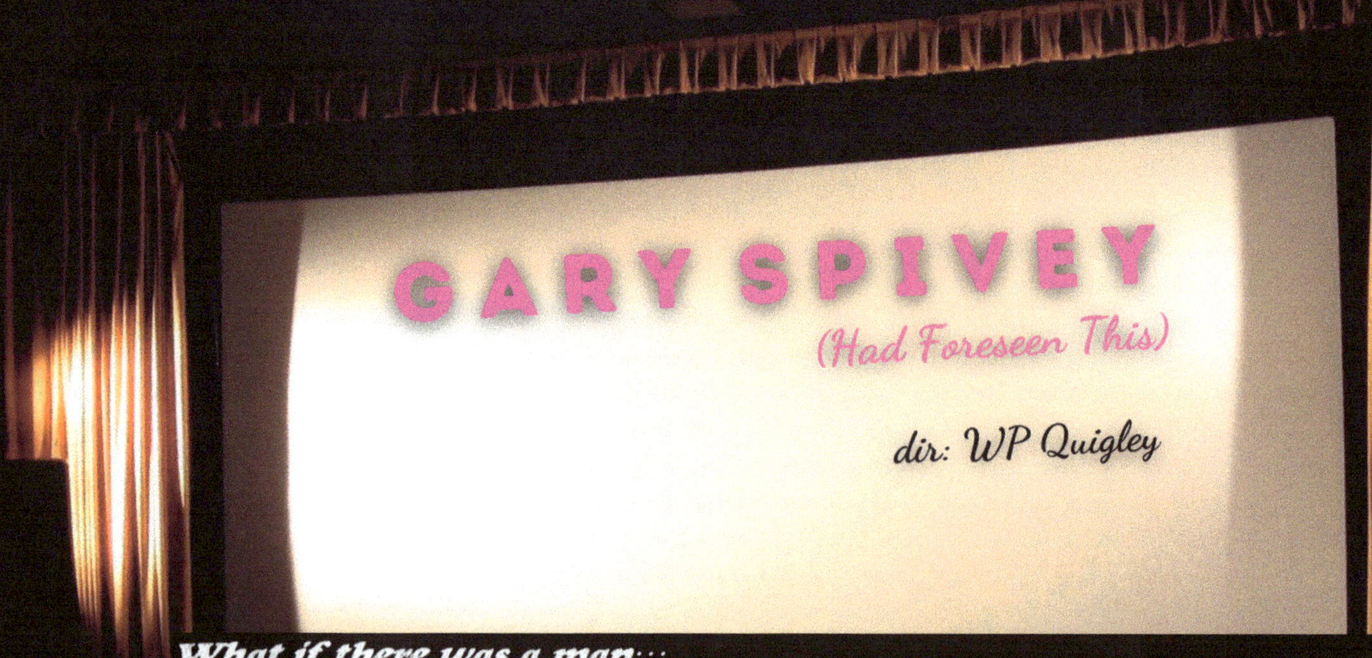

What if there was a man⋯

⋯who not only could see the future,

but who could see *until the very end?*

And what could await there⋯

⋯would it be just his end,

or the end for *all of us?*

REEL 1:
These are the people in your neighborhood...

Gary Spivey sat down on his roof, putting his Transformers lunch box down next to him as he made himself comfortable. Gary looked around and below at his once-picturesque neighborhood...at the houses and the streets and all the people running this way and that. Just four or five seconds after Gary Spivey began his survey, a gas station exploded a mile away. My, was it loud! My, was it bright! It was so bright, Gary had to shield his eyes from the blast.

Gary's arm got tired fast, though. He dropped his arm and instead looked down at his lunchbox.

There, on the side of the aluminum and rectangular pail facing up at the sky was a drawing of Optimus Prime. When Gary saw the blue and red cybernetic warrior standing ready to guard the contents of the Thermos, to defend his peanut butter sandwich, and to keep watch over his fruit snacks, Gary felt truly safe.

Gary didn't know why it was Optimus Prime, and not Duke of G.I. Joe, or Cyclops from the X-Men that made him feel so secure. Optimus Prime was the leader of the Autobots, and he protected the weak no matter what. Optimus Prime always did the right thing, even when it hurt him. Maybe that was why he made Gary Spivey feel safe. Maybe it was the cool laser guns Optimus had instead.

Feeling safe was important. You can't feel happiness unless you feel safe. His mom told him that when he was younger. Mom was always right.
When Gary Spivey went up to his roof to watch the show, every day at lunchtime, he always liked to sit on the very edge of his roof. It was so he could let his legs dangle down, so he could kick them back and forth — at first swinging them back and forth in slow, grand, sweeping movements and then as fast as he could, as if he were running on the ground. He wasn't a very fast runner on the ground. Up here, he was a champion sprinter.

He didn't know why doing that made him so happy, but it did. His mom told him that being happy was one of the most important things in life.

Gary is forty-one years old.
His mom died thirty-one years ago.

On the day she died, Gary Spivey began working it all out. "It" was everything that was going to happen for the next thirty-one years. He stopped at forty-one, because after that time, there was nothing else to work out.

Optimus Prime himself would not be able to stop what happened then.

Mr. Roper, the man who lived directly across from Gary, was what people called a 'doomsday prepper'. There was an episode of Karen, an afternoon talk show, that was dedicated to them, and Gary had watched it all three times it was on — the first time when it was a new episode, and both times it showed as a rerun. Mr. Roper wasn't on the show himself, not like Gary had been, but there were lots of people on it who were 'like' him. Those people weren't laughed at like Gary was, though. Mostly, the people in the audience were afraid of the 'doomsday preppers'. The 'doomsday preppers' talked about how the end of the world was coming, and that if people were smart, they'd be doing the same thing too. They talked about how many guns they had, how much food and water they had stored in their basements, who they would let into their 'bumpers' — wait, no, that wasn't right — 'bunkers' was what they said, and their fortifies, or forts, or whatever that word was they said. The people in the audience thought the 'doomsday preppers' were crazy, but they didn't laugh at them. The people in the audience laughed at Gary, though. But the 'doomsday preppers' were so funny, though! But Gary didn't laugh at them because they were crazy, though. They weren't crazy. Gary laughed at them because Gary knew nothing they said they did or what they were going to do would help them.

Gary stopped laughing at them though.
It wasn't nice to laugh at people.
Especially when they were scared.

The audience at the Karen show laughed at him. The laughter scared him. When the audience saw him become frightened, they laughed harder, and louder at him.

Mr. Roper had put big wooden boards on all his windows, to keep bad people out. He put big metal bars on his door, also to keep bad people out.

Gary worked out that the boards and the bars were really there to keep Mr. Roper in, but that they'd eventually stop working. Everything stops working after long enough.

The front door to Mr. Roper's house opened, and out came Mr. Roper. Gary hadn't seen Mr. Roper since last year. It was Spring, when all the soldiers in the green and brown uniforms came to America. They were from China. Gary knew that they would be coming.

Gary Spivey had foreseen this.

Mr. Roper's eyes went all squinty when he stepped out of his front door and down the two steps to his yard. Mr. Roper used to have the most beautiful, trimmed, emerald- green front lawn. Now it was all brown and yellow and weeds as tall as his chest, and Mr. Roper was tall, too. Taller than even Gary Spivey!

Mr. Roper had a scary looking gun in his hands.

He pointed it out towards the street, this way and that, but not at anything really at all.

Gary decided that the explosion at the gas station is what made the bars and the boards stop working. Mr. Roper did not have very long, Gary thought. He'd better say hi and goodbye before it was too late.

"HI MISTER ROPER!!!!" yelled Gary to his neighbor.

Gary giggled after he yelled to him. Mr. Roper had a funny name. It was just like the neighbor on Three's Company. That was a funny television show. It was okay to laugh at that show because you were supposed to laugh at it.

Mr. Roper pointed the gun at Gary Spivey. Gary wasn't afraid though. Optimus Prime was right next to him, so he was safe. Mr. Roper was an accountant. He did not know how to use the scary gun he had in his hands. Gary was double safe.

"Gary? Gary Spivey? Is-is that you?"

"Sure is, Mr. Roper! It sure is good to see you!"

Mr. Roper's eyes adjusted to the sunlight. He looked up at Gary sitting on his roof.

"How – how are you even still alive Gary?"

Mr. Roper could not believe his neighbor had survived a whole year and a half.

"Easy, Mr. Roper. I worked it all out, remember?"

"Y-yeah, Gary. I know. Did you hear that explosion just now? It sounded close. Are the chinks here?"

Chinks was a bad word. Chinks was a mean word. Gary didn't like that word.

"They're called Chinese, Mr. Roper."

"Whatever, Gary. The explosion? What was it?"

"It was the gas station, Mr. Roper. It went KA-BOOM!!" yelled Gary.

Just then, Gary noticed that to his right, the van with four colors creeping along his street.
"The gas station? Where Gary? The one by the on-ramp?"

"Yup! That's the one Mr. Roper. But you should go back inside now. The Horsemen are coming!"
Mr. Roper thought that Gary was talking about the ones from the Bible. The metaphor ones.

Gary wasn't talking about those Horsemen.
The van crept closer. Mr. Roper did not notice the van. He was busy talking to Gary Spivey. Talking, but not listening. Nobody listened to Gary.

"Gary, I need you to tell me if the gas station is on…"

One of the Horsemen, from inside the van yelled: "FIRE!!!"

There was a bang.
Mr. Roper's head snapped back, like a rubber band, pulling the rest of his body along with it. His front door was sprayed with red and goo and black chunks and clear wet stuff. Mr. Roper fell to the ground in a pile.

Gary was sad because he didn't get to say goodbye to Mr. Roper. His mom had told him that whenever he was sad, he could always sing himself a song to cheer up. So that's what Gary did.

"Come and knock on our door…we'll be waiting for you…"

The Horsemen stopped their van in between Gary's house and Mr. Roper's. Three men stepped out. Gary knew their names.

There was Ricky.
There was Chris.
And there was Stevie.
Stevie had a brother.
Gary always wanted a brother, too.

Ricky and Chris ran into the house. They were happy, laughing and giggling the whole way. They had been trying to get into Mr. Roper's house for a long time – since the Horsemen came back to the neighborhood last winter actually.

Stevie stayed outside. Stevie stared up at Gary. Gary stopped singing, smiled, and waved at him.

"Hi Stevie!" he called down to him.

Stevie just kept staring.
Gary thought it was meant to scare him.

Gary held up his lunch box in front of his face so Optimus Prime faced Stevie.

Gary cried out: "Robots in disguise!!!"

It took Ricky and Chris about two hours to fill up their van with Mr. Roper's stuff. Mostly food and water, and a lot of guns. Gary never understood the guns part though. They didn't help.

Stevie stopped staring and finally spoke.

"Let us in, you fuckin feeb queer motherfucker." Stevie pulled out a gun and pointed it at Gary. Gary was afraid, but only for a second. He had worked this part out too. It wasn't time to let them in, yet. Almost though!

17

Stevie fired a single round into the air.
"NOW,. YOU DUMB FUCKING CUNT!!"
Stevie frowned.

"Those are all very bad words, Stevie. What would your mom say if she heard you say them?"

"My mom's dead motherfucker, and so is yours! NOW LET US IN!!!"

That last made Gary frown. He missed his mom every single day. Every single day since...

"Not yet Stevie, but soon! Maybe come back tomorrow?"

Chris walked up behind Stevie and whispered in his ear. Stevie smiled. He holstered his gun.

Chris and Stevie got into the van and drove off.

There were only two people left living on Gary's street now that Mr. Roper was dead. All the people were gone, having either fled or died.

Gary took out his peanut butter sandwich and watched the fire and the smoke from the gas station rise above the rooftops and almost burn the sky. It all made him sad. Gary began to sing again, kicking his legs back and forth as they dangled off his roof.

"These are the people in your neighborhood, your neighborhood, your neighborhood!

REEL 2:
The "Karen" Show

It was three years before the People's Republic of China launched their full-scale invasion of the good ol' U.S of A, and Gary Spivey was in Los Angeles, California to try and warn people about this very thing. He was also there to try to warn them about how that event would kick off the end of humans as a species - no survivors, no stragglers, not a soul to keep.
Gary had worked all of this out years and years before, mapping out the entire future of mankind by the time he'd reached nineteen years old. He even was able to divine his eventual appearance on a massively popular, nationwide afternoon talk show. He knew no one was going to listen to him. He still had to try.

He remembered one time asking his mom why it was important to help people that didn't want to be helped or couldn't be helped. Why be nice to people who are mean to you?

His mother had said "because that's what good, kind-hearted people do, Gary. They try anyway. Because knowing, and not trying, makes you as bad as everyone else. Do you wanna be like other people?"

"No Mom. I want to be like Optimus Prime!"

Gary's mother laughed.

"Well, Optimus Prime would help people, wouldn't he?"

"Yyyyyyup!"

So Gary Spivey went to city he'd only seen on television and went on the Karen show to be just like his hero, the leader of the Autobots.

But Gary did not foresee that he would be laughed at by the studio audience, or how much, however. He also did not foresee that he would cry so much after the taping. Emotions and feelings were different; those could never be foreseen. Only the events, the things, the causes, the effects.

The day he went to the television studio, Gary was the lone guest for a taping of Karen, an hour-long program that would eventually become the number one rated afternoon talk show in America. When it did become number one and its host became a cult of personality and part of the American zeitgeist, guests like Gary Spivey were a thing of the past, replaced by A-list celebrities and asinine host and studio audience impromptu dance parties.

The eponymous Karen was Karen Severin, born Alexandra Yaeger in the year of our Lord 1976 in Boise, Idaho. She was the oldest child of four, as well as the daughter of closet Nazi sympathizer. This unsavory fact was known to her agents and her handlers and was deftly handled in a very special episode of Karen, in which she came to grips with the ignorance and hate-filled upbringing.

Yaeger, as was a far more appropriate surname to use when discussing her moral outlook and ethical stance, was the only one out of the Yaeger children to fully internalize and adopt her father's attitudes towards race, sexual orientation, and religion e.g., if a person wasn't white, Christian, and straight, that person wasn't a human being.

Yaeger changed her name when she moved to Los Angeles in the early 2010's to Karen Severin and caught on as a production designer for the Ellen show.
Like a true narcissist, she doggedly studied, analyzed, and ultimately perfected the beats of her unknowing mentor and then skillfully negotiating the daytime talk show world. Yaeger found herself at the helm of her very own show just three years later.

Ellen and the like were still very much at the top of the heap, so to speak, so the Karen show was relegated to the 2 pm timeslot – a dead zone for ratings – and on syndicated networks that played on channel 36 in one city's market, 25 in an another. Because of this, Yaeger could only manage C and D-list types of guests, the kind that Oprah pulled in during her early years:

Cult leaders with multiple wives lured in from remote compounds in Texas. Debauched filth, thought Yaeger as she interviewed an individual who had the audacity to call himself a 'reverend'.

Leaders of prominent LGBTQ organizations fighting to maintain marriage equality and equal rights in a nation that slowly – and rightfully – took their rights away. Sinners bound for the bottom pits of Perdition was the only thing that came to mind as she asked each what their hopes for American society were. Lawyers for the Jewish Defamation League, on her show to discuss the uptick in anti-Semitic violence since President Cole took office.

With each episode, Yaeger lost more and more of her patience and restraint, before restrained aggression became thinly veiled belligerence. And with each escalation of Yaeger's hostility towards the scum that was brought on her show, the more her ratings climbed and the more she became noticed by the major networks.

At last, the call came, and Yaeger, or Karen, was optioned for NBC – at 4 pm no less.

She'd hit a nerve in the general populace, that hate and ignorance-filled one that never seemed to truly depart or disappear from the American psyche.

Gary's appearance on the show was a last-second replacement, after Florida representative Doug Flatbush was forced to cancel. More underage girls had come forward in an ever-increasing scandal.

Gary dressed for the occasion, too. He wore his nice, clean white jacket and the curly white wig his mother wore to cover up the hair she'd lost through chemotherapy. His mother would always be with him that way. The wig was perfectly spherical – putting it on, it made his head appear as if it were a furry microphone head. He was very nervous – so nervous! – but his mom would be so proud of him.

"Karen Severin" introduced him to the audience and to the cameras as a self-proclaimed "psychic", "prognosticator", and "helper". The stagehand standing next to him gave him a quick nudge towards the set with her clipboard and hand.

He pointed to himself and asked the stagehand:

"Me? Is it my turn now?"

The stagehand glared at him.

"Yes, retard. Go!"

The stagehand shooed him in the same direction she'd just shoved him. Gary hesitantly walked out into the brightly lit area.

And as soon as he walked out onto the stage, the audience began snickering immediately. They were laughing at how he was dressed, and at his mom's wig. To a person, Gary Spivey looked like he was certifiably crazy and completely detached from reality. Gary sat down and looked around the studio anxiously. The lights were very very bright, so he couldn't see any of the people that had been snickering at him as he made his way to his chair.

The chair wasn't comfortable. Sitting in it in front of these people wasn't comfortable.

"Mr. Spivey, welcome to the show!"

Gary saw the host, Karen Severin, step forward and out of the bright stage lights. She was stern, angry looking woman, wearing a crimson power dress while sporting short, jet-black hair. Gary thought that she resembled a vampire from a scary movie he saw a few years before.

"Uh, hello Ms. Karen." Gary raised a right hand upwards in greeting.

"Hi Gary. Thank you for coming." Brain-damaged moron, she thought.

"Now people, our producers here on the show discovered Mr. Spivey through an online viral video that's recently surfaced on YouTube. In a manner of just a few short weeks, the video has garnered five… million…views. In the video, a much younger Gary runs down his predictions for the future of not just America, but the entire human race. Let's run the clip, please…"

The monitors above the audience first turn black, then to static. Finally the video of Gary begins. The first thing the audience notices is how much younger Gary is when the video was made; in it, he cannot be more than twenty or twenty-one years old. The second thing they notice is that he is wearing the same ivory-white spherical wig and matching dress jacket. It's as if he hasn't changed his clothes in twenty years, clothes that were hand-me-downs on whatever spaceship he rode to Earth upon. There is more giggling and laughing before he begins speaking.

The video is simply Gary seated at a desk and reading from a series of pink loose-leaf notebooks. The Karen show producers have made their own edit of the "uncut" version that had been circulating on YouTube and the internet. It is a mere five minutes long, but covered events that occurred just prior to and immediately after what would be the day of Gary's appearance on the show.

The last ten minutes of the "uncut" video was not shown.

"In 2008, the United States will elect its first black person as president. Everyone will think that it means that America isn't racist anymore, but it will make the racist people even angrier. After him, a very bad orange man will be president, and he'll make the racist people very happy."

The studio audience is dead silent with this first statement. The video was quite clearly recorded sometime in the early nineties, and with a camcorder to boot. How could this man possibly have known that O' Leary would have won the election in 2008, and that Cole would win in 2016? Already, the word "hoax" appeared in the minds of many in the studio audience.

"There's gonna be a worldwide sickness while the orange man is in charge, and it will kill a lot of people. A lot of people will be sad, but more people will be angry for some reason. Nobody likes being told what to do, even if it helps other people. That's how the end starts, though, but I'll get to that part."

"No, Alexandra, it's not the disease that starts the end. It's because empathy is dead now."

"Mr. Spivey," Yaeger laughs nervously, "my name is Karen. I don't know-"

"No, your name is Alexandra. I looked it up. Alexandra Yaeger. You changed it legally when you came to California so nobody would..."

Yaeger's face turns as white as Gary's wig and jacket. There is no hiding how livid she'd become at the mention of her real name. Already, her producers and agents were doing damage control behind the scenes.

"What could possibly mean by 'empathy is dead' Mr. Spivey? Are you saying my audience doesn't care about their neighbors, or about their friends?"

Boos erupted from the audience.
Gary became frightened.

"N-n-no, I didn't say that. I didn't say that everyone!"

Gary frowns. His mom told him something like this would happen if he tried to help.

"Well then, what did you mean, Gary?"

Gary mumbled his answer.

"Please speak up, Gary. My audience would like to know what you meant by your statement."

"People don't care about other people's feelings anymore," he replied.

Yaeger turned to her audience and rolled her eyes. There were mocking shouts from audience members.

"Oh, please," one member yelled.

"Snowflake!" yelled another.

Gary wanted to go home. Leave this awful room with its awful people and awful ringmaster and go home. He wanted to go home and see his friend Billy.

Yaeger motioned for the tape to continue. The yells from the audience silenced when it resumed.

"And then, I'll be on television! People won't like me though. People don't like me anyways, but then people will hate me. They don't like it when someone says bad stuff is going to happen, but then they really don't like it when someone like me says it. Everybody wants to be better than somebody else. Everybody wants to have more than somebody else. There will be a small group of people who have a lot more – so much more than everyone else. Five or six people will have as much as the whoooooollle world! And people won't be angry about that, though. They'll think they're just the coolest people ever. Because they had to be to get all that money. And people will think that if they're just like them, they'll be able to get as much as they do. If they work really hard and be friends with the right people they'll have way more than everyone else too!"

Yaeger interrupts again.

"So let me guess, Gary. You have a problem now with hardworking Americans?" Yeager is egging the studio audience and achieves mostly the same effect as before. There are hisses. One calls Gary a "liberal socialist commie".

But there were some, here and there in the gathered masses, that remained silent at the latest prompting for outrage. The child-like man sitting before them had known, years before, that someday he was going to be on television and had known he was going to be ridiculed for it.

The theory that Gary Spivey was perpetrating an elaborate hoax vanished for those few; dismissal and mockery disappeared in their minds. They were replaced with sympathy and concern.

One of those audience members spoke up at that moment.

"Hey! Leave him alone!"

That member, a man in his mid-thirties was immediately turned upon by those sitting around him.

Yaeger, sensing a loss of control over her audience, jumped right in.

"Gary, it appears your last statement was quite divisive. What's wrong with being hardworking?"

Gary was confused. His words had been twisted, and he didn't understand what was happening.

"I didn't say that."

"Well then, what did you say Gary?"

"What I meant was, what I was t-trying to s-say was, that the people who run our lives lie to us. But they don't always speak the lies. T-they show us lies. We believe them. Because it's nice. We want to believe them."

The crowd goes silent.

Yaeger/Karen is silent.

"I just worked it all out...everyone. I worked out all the things that were going to happen. I had to keep me and my friend Billy safe. I couldn't...I couldn't keep my mom safe. She's dead."

"Are we supposed to feel sorry for you now Gary?" asked Yaeger, trying to regain the audience. This feeb had managed to steal them from under her control.

"N-n-no. But I worked everything out that was going to happen, so I'd know if something bad was coming to get me – or Billy – again."

"And is something bad coming to get you, Gary?"

"Yes, ma'am. Something bad comes to get everyone, Alexandra."

"My name is Karen, Mr. Spivey."

"Something bad is coming to get you, too."

Gary wasn't thinking about how he sounded then. He was trying to help people, to warn them. He wasn't aware enough to realize what he had just said sounded like a threat.

The studio audience turned on him again, raining down with boos and hisses. Even the ones whom he'd elicited feelings of sympathy with.
Yaeger made silencing gestures with her hand.

"So who's my boogeyman, Mr. Spivey? What's the bad thing coming to me?"

Gary was silent. He was scared. He was sweating through his shiny white spherical wig. He was sweating through his shiny white dress jacket.

"It happens on the day that China invades America, Ms. Yaeger. It happens right here, in your studio. Nobody is loved more than you when it does. You're at big awards shows with big celebrities a couple of weeks before. But then it's over."
Yaeger is silent for a moment, but then laughs at him.

"Mr. Spivey, I was willing to give you the benefit of the doubt, but it is

clear that you are a scam artist and a fake."

The audience joins in with her laughter, and as the taping cuts to a commercial break, it reaches a peak.
Yaeger turns to the camera closest to her.
"We'll be right back to wrap up with uh..Mr. Spivey here. Don't go away."

The red light on top of the camera that indicated when it was recording went dark. But the laughter continued.

"I want to go see my friend Billy now, Ms. Yaeger."

Yaeger heard his plea, and with the cameras and the microphones off, she casually strolled up to Gary, leaned in close to him and said:

You call me Yaeger one more time, and I'll have you fucking shot before you get back to your hotel room."

Gary fell backwards on his seat to the floor, scrambled to his feet, and ran. He could hear the studio audience continue to laugh at him as he disappeared off stage left. The entire time he ran, Gary just kept repeating over and over…

"I'm gonna go see Billy, my friend. I'm gonna go see Billy, my friend. I'M GONNA GO SEE BILLY, MY FRIEND!!!"

The audience joins in with her laughter, and as the taping cuts to a commercial break, it reaches a peak.

Yaeger turns to the camera closest to her.

"We'll be right back to wrap up with uh..Mr. Spivey here. Don't go away."

The red light on top of the camera that indicated when it was recording went dark. But the laughter continued.

REEL 3: Bedtime Stories

Gary stayed up the roof for a few hours after the Horsemen left. He sang "People in Your Neighborhood" a couple times, but it wasn't enough to stave off the sadness and loneliness he felt after he saw Mr. Roper killed. There was something about the knowledge that there was another person still living nearby - still in the house or home they'd resided in before the world unraveled, that was reassuring, comforting. This feeling was there regardless of whether that person ever left their house, showed their face in a window, or even turned on an upstairs light occasionally.

Mr. Roper did none of these, and hadn't in a long, long time. It didn't matter. He was dead. His body would lay in an awkward position on his front steps until it wasted away completely.

When he'd finished singing, Gary couldn't help but recall the time he'd been on tv, when he'd gone to Los Angeles and been on that awful woman's television show. It was seeing Mr. Roper get shot that reminded him of that time – because the very same thing had happened to the Yaeger woman. She hadn't been home when it did, not like Mr. Roper, but her head had snapped back in exact same way as his dead.

It had been on live television when it did

Gary, of course, knew it was going to happen.

He tried to tell her while he was on her show, tried to warn her.
She didn't like it when he had and neither did all the people in the studio.

It took a couple of years, but Gary finally realized that she and all of the people there thought he was threatening her.

As if he could actually do something horrible like that.

Gary couldn't hurt a fly.

Moreover, Gary wouldn't hurt a fly. They were God's creatures too, after all. Gary's revisit of that day ended with his exit from the studio, running for the exit and yelling that he wanted to go home and see his friend. It made him want to go see his friend in the present as well. Gary and his friend were the only people left on his street and Gary didn't want to feel lonely anymore. It was a terrible thing to have to feel.

Gary packed up his garbage from his lunch into his Transformers lunchbox, stood up carefully to not fall off his roof, and then made his way to the skylight he used to get up there in the first place.

Billy was downstairs in the living room, watching a VCR cassette of G.I. Joe. That Billy. He always watched G.I. Joe. Gary always wondered why he didn't like Transformers, or any of the other cartoons they had on cassettes. Maybe it was because Billy wanted to be a soldier too, once. Maybe he just liked the guns.

When Gary had first met Billy, he had a gun just like the Joes, and Cobra did.
Gary walked down the stairs and Billy jumped up from the couch as he did.

"Gary!! I heard them knocking at the door!! Is it time? Just like you said?"

Gary stopped at the bottom and smiled boyishly.

"Now Billy, if I've told you once, I've told you a thousand times. When it's time, I'll tell you."

Gary sounded like a loving, patient, but somewhat exasperated parent just then. Billy's question was one he'd clearly had to answer many, many times before. Gary walked over to Billy and mussed his hair the way a father does to a son, as a sign of affection and reassurance.

"But when that time comes, what did I say was going to happen?"

Billy grinned from ear to ear.

"YOOOOOOOO JOE!!!!!" Billy exclaimed.

"That's right buddy!"

Gary felt immediately better for having come downstairs, yet still a little sad. The 'time' that Gary and Billy were discussing was tomorrow morning. But it was okay, though. Because Gary knew that he'd never have to be lonely – or scared – ever again when it was done.

Gary Spivey had foreseen this.

Gary went to their kitchen to clean up. There were only a few morsels of food left in the house, just enough to make it through that night. But this was fine – they wouldn't need more than what they had. Still, Gary had to make sure Billy was fed and happy and ready.

"Are you hungry, Billy?" exclaimed Gary.

The television in the living room was turned up too loud for Billy to hear him though, so Gary made his way back to the living room, where Billy had resumed watching his favorite cartoon.

He stopped short at the open archway between the two rooms, catching a look at the patch of skin at the back of Billy's head where no hair had grown for years and years. Poor, poor Billy.

But then again, Billy was so mean and scary before Gary's mom was able to hit him there. What was it she had used again? Oh yes. The iron she used to press Gary's dress shirts for school. There was so much blood when she hit him there!

"Billy?"

His head spun around faster than a freshly released top.

"Yes buddy?"

"Are you hungry? I was going to make you your dinner now."

"YYYYYup! Can I have soup again?"

That Billy. He loved his GI Joe, and he loved his soup.

"You sure can, little man!" Gary smiled at Billy.

Billy smiled back. They both went about their activities.

Gary returned a few moments later, placing the bowl of Campbell's Chunky Beef in front of him on the tv tray. He sat up from his reclined position on the couch, and greedily began devouring the concoction.

It was the last can of soup they had.

After finishing, Gary saw that his friend was very sleepy. Soup always seemed to do that to him, regardless of the time of day.

Knowing this (Gary did not need his knack for precognition in this circumstance), Gary stayed close to his friend, seated next to him on the couch, ready to make good on what Billy always asked him after finishing his soup.

Billy put his feet up on the opposite end of the couch and his head down on Gary's leg. He pulled a blanket over himself and then stuck his thumb into his mouth.

"Will you tell me the story again, Gary?"

The story was always different, because Billy couldn't really remember very much anymore — other than what he had to do when the 'time' came. There was one story, however, that Gary told far more than all the others.

It was how he made sure Billy knew what to do when the 'time' came.

"Okay, buddy. Close your eyes! Bedtime story!"

Billy did as he was told.

"This is the story of the Four Horsemen, and how they heralded the end of the world...."

Gary spoke the last part of the sentence in an ominous tone, as if to initiate a spooky campfire tale.

Billy moaned and stirred in his near-fetal position. He settled in quickly thereafter.

Gary began.

"Once upon a time, there was a boy, his mom whohelovedverymuch, and four young men. These men liked to call themselves The Four Horsemen..."

And so began the last bedtime story ever told in the history of mankind.

Or, at least the part that Gary Spivey had foreseen.

Four horsemen of the apocalypse.

Billy, Steve, Ricky, and Chris had always run together since they had met in high school, since they had all dropped out together, and for the ensuing couple of years afterwards. They had been the town ne'er-do-wells and taken quite a bit of pride in filling that role. Once each had run into their own personal share of trouble with local authorities, ranging from destruction of property, underage drinking, assault, to things more serious and permanently life damaging, the four of them decided to become their own self-styled 'gang', as much as that were possible in the suburb in which they lived. They called themselves, prosaically enough, "The Horsemen", because there were four of them and they were badasses and they were not to be messed with.

To wit, none of them had thought to designate themselves as famine, death, war, or plague as is described in the Bible.

They simply stayed with Billy, Steve, Ricky, and Chris.

Steve and Billy also happened to be twins, of the fraternal type, but they still bore an uncanny resemblance to each other. So much so, they allowed people to think they were identical.

It came upon them, in one particularly asinine group discussion on one particularly asinine afternoon, to rob someone. One should note here that they chose not to rob a store, thinking that they would be much more easily caught if they had done so. Instead, they chose to break into someone's house, and rob the owners. Gary and his mother, and the house in which they lived, were chosen as targets.

The asinine justification for doing so was the knowledge that Mr. Spivey had left his wife and developmentally disabled son years before, so there would be no husband to present resistance to their caper. This would make matters much easier, once again.

The four of them chose the middle of the day to make their assault, believing that most everyone on the street would be either at work or busy with their daily routines. Doors would not be locked and the Spiveys would be caught unsuspecting.

Again, The Horseman believed this was a smart move.

They were correct in that Mrs. Spivey would be caught unsuspecting — it was a safe neighborhood, at least up until that point.

Their plan, however, fell apart when not a single member anticipated that Mrs. Spivey was in fact, a former marine.

At exactly noon, the four Horsemen pulled up in front of Gary's house in the very same van they would decades later, after the proverbial "shit" had not hit the fan but had been scattered about the room in a shit-splatter pattern.

The four of them ran in through the front door and proceeded about their "robbery".

It went about as well as one would think.

Gary was a mere ten years old at that time, was sat in the living room. He'd been watching Transformers when the front door came flying inwards with Horsemen pouring in one after the other.

They'd decided upon ski masks to hide their faces but neglected to avoid using their first names when shouting to each other for the next hour or so.

Dolores had barely been able to make ends meet let alone possess 'valuables'.

Upon reuniting with his cohorts, Steve gave the signal for their collective departure. Billy, however, decided that he had not gotten all he had came for.

"Now let's just wait a second, there big bro. I think Mrs. Spivey has something else to give us…"

At which point, Billy began to unbutton his jeans.

Ricky spoke immediately. This was not part of their plan. Not at all.

"Billy, come on. We gotta get the fuck out of here. Somebody might have seen us come in."

Ricky was correct in his assertion. The police were already on their way.

Billy became distracted by Ricky's whining, and when he was, he dropped his unloaded firearm to the ground.

"Goddamnit," he mumbled, and bent down to retrieve it from the ground.

Dolores saw that his weapon was not only unloaded (there was no magazine present in his gun), assumed that none of these idiots were truly packing, and seized her chance.

She brought the iron down as hard she could onto the back of his skull, striking it with the point of the appliance. Her blow cracked his skull open and knocked him unconscious instantly.

Gary looked over his mother after she'd done this. From his position at the bottom of the stairs, Steve fired four bullets into Dolores, knocking her backwards. Gary counted each crimson hole that tore into his mother's blouse as they appeared.

One.
Two.
Three.
Four. Four!

The approaching sirens were heard by all at that moment, and Chris exclaimed: "LET'S FUCKING GO!!!"

Steve made for his brother, but Ricky grabbed him by his arm.

"Forget him, man, there's nothing we can do."

"He's my fucking brother man!!"

"LET'S GO, STEVE," and Ricky dragged him out the door. The remaining three horsemen escaped just as the police arrived. Rather than stopping and entering the crime scene, the cruiser first on the scene pursued the perpetrators instead.

Gary went to his mother, gasping for air in the last moments of her life.

He asked: "What should I do, Mommy?"

"He-he-help…." was all she could manage.

Gary thought that what she was trying to say was to "help even those who are mean to us", like he would recall time and time again over his life.

She was merely trying to say, "help me," of course.

Gary left her where she lay, instead trying to help Billy, in his own misguided way.

Gary thought she'd meant for him to help Billy. So he did what he thought he was supposed to.

Using all of his might, Gary pushed the unconscious Billy underneath their couch, and hid him from the police, first responders, and so on that arrived moments later. And somehow, Billy had not been found, assumed to have fled with his cohorts.

Later, when Gary was returned home, under the care of his Auntie Sophie, managed to "help" Billy.

Billy became his friend, having sustained severe cerebral trauma and rendered into a child-like state for the remainder of his days.

Gary turned eighteen, was deemed fit to look after himself in the house in which he lived, and that was that.

To prevent and anticipate anything like what happened on that day from ever happening again, Gary began to work everything out. Everything that could - or would- ever happen again.
Because to be happy, you had to feel safe. Mom had said that to Gary once, too.

Gary's retelling of this tale was a bit more fairy tale than above, but the highpoints and the crucial details were all still there. Once Gary had it all worked out, he'd added another chapter to round out the story.

Because all bedtime stories had to have a happy ending.

REEL 5: Robots in disguise! YOOOO JOE!!

Gary fell asleep in the same seat on the couch he sat in when he guided his buddy to sleep the night before. He opened his eyes, rubbed the sleep out of them, and let out a protracted yawn.

It was 'time'.

He gently shook Billy awake, whose head had shifted from his it's initial resting place upon his leg and into a snug nook of the couch, in between two cushions.

"Billy...Billy...time to wake up."

"N-n-no. More sleep for Billy," Billy mumbled, half-asleep.

"Hey Billy, guess what."

"Mmmmm?"

"It's time."

Billy's eyes popped open, as if he'd been shocked with electricity.

"REALLY BUDDY?!!?"

"Yep. Time to get ready."

"YOOOO JOE!!!"

Billy shot up from his horizontal position and ran into the basement.
Gary called after him: "Robots in disguise!"

Gary heard the van pull up out front. He stood up from the couch, stretched to work out the kinks in his back from the sitting position he slept the night in, and walked to the front door. He lifted the metal bar from its hook, and proceeded to unlock the six or seven locks, deadbolts, and other security devices that had been installed on them years before. Gary knew he'd need all of that in place years before the world began to burn, because of course...

Gary Spivey had foreseen this.

Once all had been opened, Gary even went so far as to open the front door. He saw Steve, Ricky, and Chris begin to exit the van, and even waved to them before returning to the living room proper.

He kept singing as he did so.

"Autobots wage their battle to destroy the evil of...THE DECEPTICONS," the last bit spoken in a pseudo-robotic voice for emphasis.

Gary smiled as he heard the approaching footsteps from outside. His smile broadened when he heard the footsteps of Billy running up the basement steps.

It was all as he had foreseen.

Gary's mother, before marrying his father, was a marine. She'd kept...mementos of her days as a soldier, for reasons that only she could be able to relate.

Maybe it was a collector's thing, maybe they were reminders of days gone by, or maybe it had been just cool to have them.

She'd been powerless to stop Gary's idiot father from abandoning them both within a week of the Doctor's diagnosis that Gary, although developmentally challenged, exhibited classic signs of "savant"- like behavior.

She'd never live to see the film Rain Man, but this was in fact what was at play with young Gary. Maybe keeping two strings of high-powered grenades in the basement restored some sense of power to her countenance.

The Horsemen entered the living room.

Gary's last words were the last words of the Transformers theme song, also spoken in a pseudo-robotic voice:

"Robots in disguise!"

Steve saw his brother's kidnapper standing in the living room, stupidly grinning. He didn't hesitate in gunning the man in the snow-white dress shirt that wore a perfectly spherical and also snow-white wig down in a hail of bullets from the AR-47 he brandished.

Gary fell to the ground, dead, with the knowledge he would never be afraid, he would never be alone, and he would never be laughed at ever again.

He was still smiling when his life passed from his body.

When Steve had finished firing, the door to the basement burst open, and out came Billy. Steve also managed a relieved smile at first sight of his long-lost brother.

And then he saw the look on Billy's face.

The smile vanished. In that moment, he knew that his brother, the fourth Horseman, had died long, long, long ago.

Flanking him were Chris and Ricky.

Ricky blurted out: "What…"
Before Billy shouted: "YOOOOOOOO JOE!!!!!!!!!"

The entire array of grenades on his shoulders had all been armed to explode and did just that as Billy reached the long "o" sound of his erstwhile war cry.

The four horsemen were all vaporized in that instant.

The end of the world was finished.

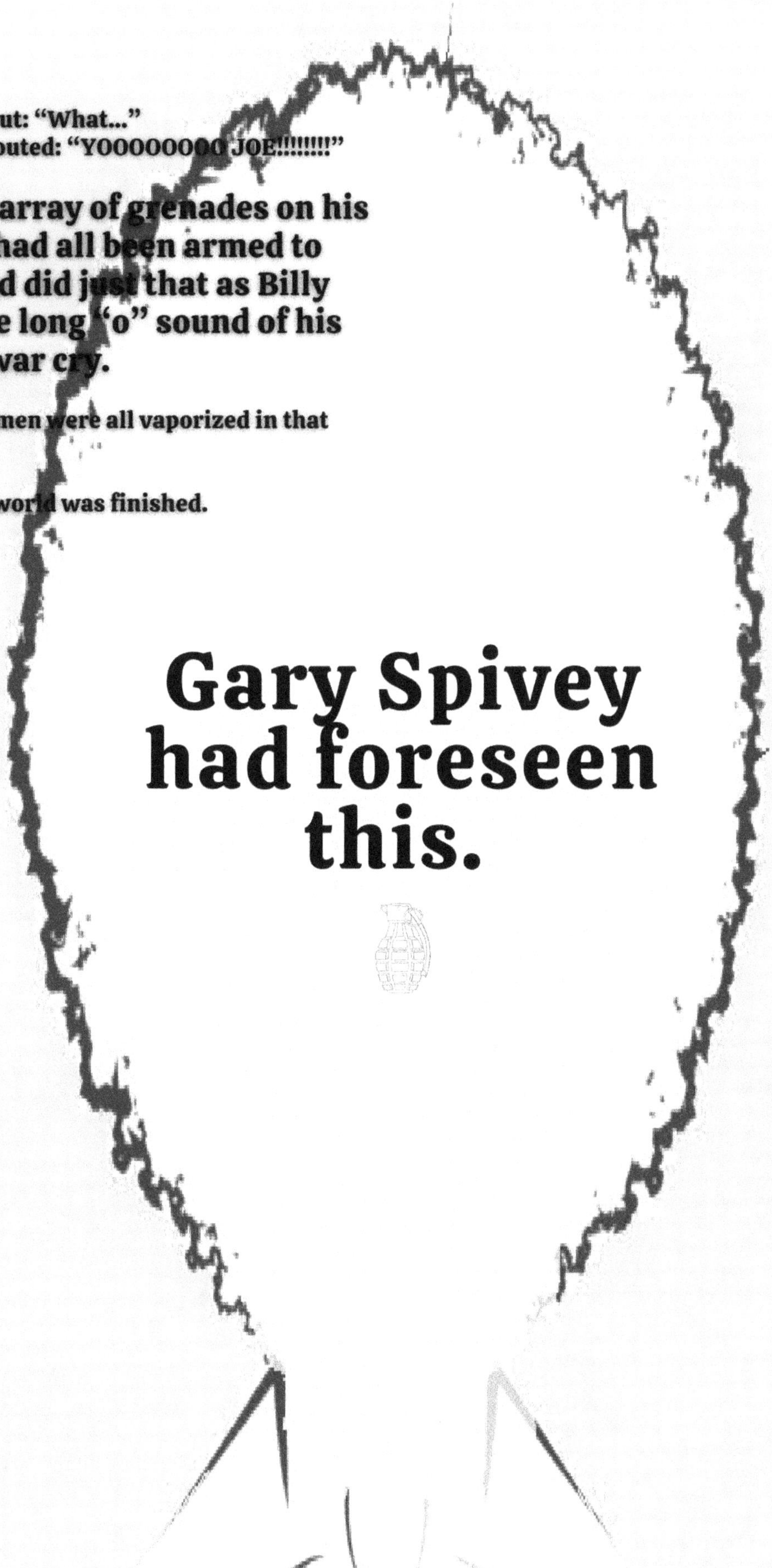

Gary Spivey had foreseen this.

WHY THE FUCK DO WE EAT POPCORN AT THE MOVIES?

DOUBLE FEATURE ASKS THE HARD-HITTING QUESTIONS...

Alright kids. Time to get those asses up from your seats, stretch, and make your collective way herd-style to our refreshment stand to help yourself to any of our (your) snacks. With any luck, you've got some microwave popcorn stashed somewhere in your kitchen, maybe a secret drawer with candy and or chocolates tucked away in. Hey, now there's a thought.

Why the fuck did popcorn become such an integral part of that uniquely American ritual that is a night out at the movies?

Would you believe it started because of the rampant illiteracy of the United States near the end of the nineteenth century? That it was cemented as the pillar it is today because of the Great Depression?

Yes? Um, okay. Well fuck you. I'm gonna tell you why anyway because trust me - you're gonna need this break before our second feature.

About thirty years before popcorn had primarily been the mainstay of outdoor attractions, e.g., the circus, fairs, and sporting events. The steam-powered popcorn maker had been invented in 1885, and because you could bring the machine basically anywhere, it was perfect for those types of events.

But at the time, theatres wanted to maintain a more high-brow, exclusive clientele; establishments that showed films wanted to remain as exclusive locations for more affluent, more refined, and mostly, more educated patrons.

Theatres (even to this day) had carpets, curtains, and a veneer of elegance about them. Translation: movie theatres weren't for poor people, who generally couldn't read anyway. Popcorn was a huge no-no in that regard.

Keep in mind, films did not have sound until 1927, so the functionally illiterate wouldn't be found in theatres regardless.

When the bold invention of "audio" became a reality, that changed. Movies could be enjoyed by anyone, the financially challenged included. In addition, the sound from the movies served to drown out the sound of people munching away on popped corn.
Movie theatres, generally speaking, did not budge. When patrons would check their coats upon entering whatever establishment, would also have to check their popcorn.
Wait, what?

Enterprising vendors, in response to theatre owners obstinance, would set up shop immediately outside theatres and take advantage of foot traffic to sell popcorn.
And then, the Great Depression forced theatres' hands.
Profits, and attendance, plummeted. Nobody had money to go to theatres anymore, and so theatres needed a cheap to produce snack to continue luring anyone with the disposable income to come to their theatres.

The theatres that sold popcorn were able to save themselves from going under. Those that didn't went under

Double Feature
10:00 pm (Presentation 2):

What will truly lead to our downfall?

Ignorance. Greed. Depravity. Savagery.

These things form just fragments

Of our total capacity for atrocity…

…in all its forms.

What possible final form could atrocity take?

CONTENT WARNING

ONE.

Arnie hadn't left his MetaPod in days.

How many had that been, exactly?

Arnie hadn't a clue.
Didn't care, either.

His mind and his senses had been fully engaged by the latest release from Amazon BioWare, Jungle Adventure 3. It had hit the MetaPod Online Store the previous weekend and had surpassed a billion in sales since its' release worldwide in retail locations.
Of course, as soon as Arnie had caught a mere glimpse of the neon green, yellow, and orange logo of the Jungle Adventure series icon in the spot where it usually appeared in the first menu screen (the MetaPod Online Store was always eye level when a user first logged in), Arnie downloaded it straight away.
For months before its launch, Jungle Adventure 3 had been touted as THE fully immersive gaming experience of the year by game, art, and culture critics all over the world.

Beginning the game, each player customized their 'avatar' as they wished – although the player ultimately saw very little of themselves once they'd been thrust into the action.

Players could build knockoffs of retro characters like Lara Croft or Sam Drake, or newer ones like Jack Powell or Alexandra Chess. There were no limits – even if the player decided to go in the direction of wish fulfillment, or of the ridiculous, with hyperbolic and exaggerated versions of themselves and their own features.
With so many possibilities for juvenile perversion at his fingertips, Arnie hadn't hesitated to build obscenely large breasts into his avatar's appearance to then eschew any kind of shirt or similar covering for those sweet ass guns he'd installed...
At every lull in the action since he'd been playing, Arnie made it a point to play patty-cake with his virtual gazongas.
Each time, he mused to himself the following mantra:
"If I can touch 'em and I can feel 'em, then they're real enough."
This was usually followed with an ample supply of giggling.

The action parts were a far, far different experience for young Arnie than his periodic exercises in self-love.

The Jungle Adventure series of games had never held the most intriguing subject material (given their choice, most gamers wanted space, shooters, or zombie games), but what this game lacked in general appeal, it more than made up for in pure realism.

It was very much as if the person jacked into the hardware was leaping from vine to vine, outracing and avoiding foes – from evil rivals in pursuit of the same treasures to belligerent natives, incensed not only at the intrusions by the player into their forbidden and sacred territory but also their wonton theft of their most revered and priceless treasures.

Arnie could not get enough of the smells he detected in those deep, dark, overgrown jungles; the way he found himself squinting when the South American sun caught an angle through the canopy directly into his vision, or the feel of the leaves as they brushed on his skin or the droplets of warm basin rain as they stuck his cheek.

He felt alive.
He felt in control.

T W O .

Arnie hadn't left his MetaPod in three days, thirteen hours, and forty-seven minutes.

He'd obviously been playing Jungle Adventure 3 for the duration, but one asks how such a thing could even be possible in the first place. Humans still required sustenance, restful sleep, and the occasional jettisoning of excess cargo, so to speak. Since it was ultimately profitable to do so, the inventors of the MetaPod also designed technology to accommodate all three biological functions in such a manner as to allow the player to continue engaging with the product with zero interruption.

Prosthetics could be purchased from Meta at their usual prohibitive and outrageous prices, one for each biological process to maximize profit.

Surgery was performed and billed to a player's health insurance (it took some doing to coax companies to cover such frivolous operations, but money was money and Meta ensured their counterparts in the healthcare industry got their cut of it. When all was said and done, Arnie could have spent an additional three days, thirteen hours, and forty-seven minutes playing in his MetaPod — and even then, he could have kept right on going until the nutrient supply had depleted entirely while either chasing down the lost temple of the Yanomamo or retrieving the Sacred Stones of the Yacuna if he'd liked.

Or playing with his giant virtual tits under a tree - if that's what caught his fancy. Arnie wouldn't get that chance again, as unbeknownst to him, Susan and Carl Sedgewick had arrived home early from their annual cross-country trip. Carl, Arnie's father, called out to him exactly twice before deducing where his son was. He stomped up the main stairs to his son's bedroom and pushed open the door.

Just playing within his MetaPod was not an infraction worthy of punishment for Arnie. The Sedgwicks were an affluent family, having been one of the few families in their neighborhood that could afford all the previously mentioned biological and mechanical accoutrements. However, very clear ground rules had been set forth when his MetaPod was first upgraded to feed him liquified protein, fats, and carbohydrates through one tube and pull the leftovers out of him through another.

One of those rules had been that Arnie Sedgewick was not to spend a second longer within the confines of the gaming device for longer than twenty-four hours. Doing so meant immediate forfeiture of MetaPod privileges, indefinitely. Carl walked to the shiny, sleek, oblong gray pod in the middle of his son's room and glanced at the time counter display installed on the outside shell (another upgrade, another exorbitant sum spent).

Carl Sedgewick had attended anger management classes once upon a time. He'd also played seven seasons for the New England Patriots as an outside linebacker. Grabbing the outside handle of the entry door, Carl tore it free with ease in his rage. Doing so meant that Jungle Adventure 3 did not have a chance to shut down properly, and so Carl caught a quick look of the actual state of the game - and his son - before the interior turned black.

Carl couldn't be sure but later, he could have sworn that his son had been playing with computer-generated fake tits and giggling to himself.

T H R E E .

The scream and shout fest that ensued upon Carl Sedgwick's rage-fueled wreckage of his son's MetaPod entry door lasted for about a half-hour and could be heard for three houses in either direction on their street.

Hank Murray, a retired author that had lived alone since his mid-forties occupied the home next door to the Sedgwicks. He'd been quietly finishing the third book in a trilogy he'd started years ago when heard the yelling next door. Hank had grown up in a family rife with abuse and neglect, so the shouting itself wasn't enough to take him out of his focus and rhythm. But after a few minutes of standard-issue arguing he heard Carl, the neighborhood's best contender for 'most likely to commit domestic assault' and neighbor he avoided at all costs bellow out:

"And did I catch you playing with yourself and your computer tits when I pulled open that door, you little pervert?"

There was total silence from his son after that, which meant yes, that was in fact the case.

"Oh fucking good god," said Hank, furrowing his eyebrows and grimacing from both the statement and the mental image it conjured.
Hank stood up from his desk, abandoned his work for the time being, and left his house entirely.

"The fuck ever happened to just knuckling one out to a video on PornHub, kids gotta simulate scenarios with MetaPods," Hank mumbled to himself while walking out his front door. He jumped into his truck, peeled out of his driveway, and fled the neighborhood as fast as he could.

Susan Sedgwick heard Hank's truck peel out following her husband's digital masturbation accusation of their son. The color drained out of her face, knowing that their neighbor had absolutely heard that portion of the argument, at least.

She'd sat on the sidelines up until that point, content to let Carl handle Arnie. But once it became damaging to her family's perception, especially on the street where they lived, Susan stepped into the fray.

Truth was, she didn't give a shit about Arnie or Carl's reputation - but she very much cared about her own.

This meant that her family was included by proxy as a statement of her ability as a wife and mother. She'd been in competition, locked into an unspoken and passive-aggressive battle with the other matriarchs on their street since they moved in fifteen years before. Anytime something controversial happened within any of their families, the rest of the women would invariably hear about it, make cruel and callous judgements about that woman behind her back, and always overcompensate with saccharine encouragement and disingenuous support to her face.

Susan made the effort to exert control over her family to be able to face down the other women in her twice monthly book club. She'd been the talked-about one too many times already because of Carl, then Arnie grew up and began weirding out all the girls his age in their circles, which only added to Susan's shame.

And under absolutely no circumstances would she end up like that idiot, Barbara Newcomb.

It was by this social dynamic that the actual leading candidate for 'most likely to commit domestic assault' wasn't Carl, but Susan Sedgwick.

Carl may have intimidated the shit out of Hank Murray with his six-foot-five, 270-pound frame, but the Lilliputian presence of Susan never failed to back the giant down whenever she had a mind to do so. The five-foot-zero, barely one-hundred-pound Susan almost tiptoed into the living room where Carl stomped and Arnie sat while Carl stomped, got in front of her husband, reached up, grabbed her husband's shirt by the open collar, and yanked him downwards into her face.

"Keep. Your. Fucking. Voice. Down. Hank Murray next door just heard your weird fucking announcement about Arnie's jerk-off routine."

It was then Carl's turn to have his face drained of its color.
The man who'd broken the single season record for sacks in 2062 was frightened to pieces of his wife, and looked as if he was going to piss his pants that very second.

"S-s-sorry, Sooz."

"Finish this. Send him to go hang out with Hilary and Adrienne."

"The Newcomb girls?"

Susan's response was an icy stare at the man as if to simultaneously say, "what the hell do you think, stupid?" and fire twin death lasers into his frontal cortex.

Susan made to exit the room. She'd effectively terminated the argument, as well as any traces of masculinity in the living room.
Once Carl had regained his composure, he cleared his throat and sat down next to his son.

"Look, I'm sorry for yelling. But you can't spend your life escaping from the real world. Your mom and I…"

(despise each other and only stay together because we had you)

"can be a little tough to handle sometimes, and I get that, but there's more to life than just…"

(long-dead, failed marriages and bullshit social statuses)

"video games, bud."

"But Dad…"

"No buts, Arnie. You heard your mother. Give the Newcomb girls a call – Adrienne is the one in your grade, right? Yeah. And go hang out with some actual people instead of computer-generated ones. Do you some good."

"Dad. Adrienne and Hilary are…"

"What? Girls?"

No. I like hanging out with girls, Dad. It's just that they…"

"They what, Arn?"

"They hate my guts, Dad."

F O U R.

Adrienne fired the remaining half of her poppy seed bagel directly at the back of her sister's head, landing a direct hit with enough force for Hilary to grab the impact site in pain. It was only a bagel, however, and not, say, a rock like Adrienne wished it was. The doughy composition was not enough to inflict the pain Adrienne desired, even in its delicious, toasted state. It was all she had to throw, however.

And it was not enough to deter Hilary from yanking out Adrienne's favorite DVD, a show from forever ago called Gossip Girls. Hilary didn't even bother putting the shiny disc back into its case, either.

Instead, she laid it down on the side that contained the disc information needed to play the video. Hilary then put in her DVD of a show called Ridiculousness, that was one idiot on a stage introducing home video clips of other idiots hurting or embarrassing themselves.

Despite it being an emotionally and intellectually stunted program, it was still pretty funny and Hilary couldn't get enough of it.

Adrienne got up from their off-blue and threadbare living room couch, pissed off to no discernible end, and delivered the kind of damage a bagel could not with a sharp backhand to Hilary's left ear.

"What part of 'I was watching that' didn't you get, bitch?"

Hilary turned, and the look she had upon her face spoke of violence and murder in only the way an enraged fourteen-year-old girl's could.

"Oh. It's on now."

Hilary leapt at her older sister like a jaguar striking at prey from its chosen cover. Adrienne anticipated her younger counterpart's move, and deftly feigned to her right.

The Newcomb sisters were once again locked in battle, just one of countless others, in their endless struggle for total dominance.

F I V E.

"…poor." finished Arnie.

His father raised an eyebrow at this last statement from his son.

"Not sure I like that, Arn. It wasn't so long ago that the Newcombs lived right here, in this very same neighborhood with us. You didn't have a problem playing with them then."

"Yeah, but Dad. It smells like shit…"

"Don't swear, Arn."

"…like garbage where they live. And there's nothing to do down at their house. Adrienne and Hilary's Dad still hasn't got a job yet and the guy drinks like a fish. They've got this thing called a DVD player that they watch movies and shows on. That's all they have, too. No video games, either. Sooooo boring…"

Carl frowned.

When he was sixteen, he spent his afternoon hurling his body at tackle dummies while a similarly anger-challenged white man screamed obscenities and insults at him. He'd have given his left testicle to have had the chance to go hang out with a couple of girls on an afternoon instead of football practice.

His son had just whined to him about the lack of video games and other electronic distractions.

Carl began to wonder where and when it was exactly he went wrong with raising his son.

"Alright, well Arn? Like I just said you're…"

Before he could finish repeating his admonishment regarding the richness of experience to be found in life, Carl's cell phone began to vibrate in his pocket.

"Hold on," he said.

I'm not done with you yet, man."

Carl stood up, pulled the device out from his pant leg and looked at the display screen. Peter Newcomb, it said. He gestured towards his son with his phone.

"Speak of the devil," he said.

"Huh?" replied Arnie.

It was a colloquialism he was unfamiliar with.

Carl turned his back to his son and hit the answer button on his cellphone.

"Pete! How you doing big guy?"

The voice on the other end began to speak. Carl found himself frowning again. The voice on the other end mumbled two sentences before Carl could tell that the man had been drinking that day.

Pete hadn't been the same since…well since Barbara's suicide. Pete had fallen to pieces without had decided to take an early exit from life. Carl felt sorry for the guy. And in that same swell of pity and empathy for Pete, Carl felt his anger rise in that same tide of emotion. His wife had been driven to make that decision out of shame – the shame she'd felt after falling out of the good graces of the women in this fucking neighborhood.

"Oh yeah? Well we were about to send Arnie over there anyway. You, uh…you okay Pete? No, just asking, you know. Uh-hunh. Well I was just gonna take Arnie down there anyway. They did what? How?"

Carl laughed at the answer to 'how' Pete gave. "Maybe I should take them to anger management class with me, then?" More laughter.

"Alright, well, I'll be down with Mr. Fix-It here in a half-hour. Yep. Alright, brother. Bye."

Arnie heard all of this and rightly assumed that he now had a secondary reason for going to the shitty part of town , one that directly related to his rudimentary skill with fixing electronics.

"Mr. Fix-It?" Arnie asked.

Carl put his phone back into his pocket, deciding whether to bring his teenager to a house where the adult had been drinking.
As she could hear him thinking from the kitchen, Susan called out to him at that exact moment.

"Hey hon? When are you two leaving for the Newcombs? The girls are going to be here in an hour and I need you to help get the place ready!"

That's where it went wrong with Arnie, Carl thought. We never solved the problems with him. We just made them go away.
He shook his head in disapproval, but not of his son. It was of he and Susan's parenting.

"C'mon Arn. The girls broke that DVD player you were just talking about. Go get that stuff you use to fix your video game systems and meet me outside. I'll get the car started."

"Dad, do I have…"

Carl felt his anger pin immediately at the continued whining.

He glared at his son.

Arnie saw the look his father gave and dropped his protest.

"Fine," he said.

The two of them were off to the Newcomb house within minutes.

S I X .

Adrienne and Hilary were laughing hysterically by the broken DVD player laying on the floor nearby. It didn't seem as if breaking the device had bothered either of them, even though they had damaged it brawling over which DVD to watch.

In the battle that ensued over Ridiculousness vs. Gilmore Girls, there had been no clear winner between shows, as there was no way to watch either in the current state of the DVD player. It did appear, at least to an impartial observer, that both Adrienne and Hilary had won.

"Kicked your ass, girl," said Adrienne in between gasps for breath.

"No fucking way," disagreed Hilary.

Adrienne backhanded Hilary across her shoulder, a mere tap compared to the fisticuffs earlier. Hilary responded with one of her own, equal in strength. They exchanged a smile.

A moment later, they heard the disordered thumping of their father upstairs, first across the living room, then to their kitchen. The door to the basement opened and then the two sisters saw the sneakers of their father coming down the basement stairs.

What-what the hell is going on down here? I heard all kinds a' commotions down here."

Adrienne, being the older of the two Newcomb girls, spoke up. She was growing used to the role of deflecting interactions with the drunk version of her father away from Hilary.

"It's nothing, Dad. We were just messing around. We weren't serious."

Hilary whispered under her breath.

"I was…"

Adrienne gave her sister a quick glance as if to say, "not now".

Their father eyed them through vodka-glazed eyes. They were suspicious eyes, but not at all from the emotion or feeling of being suspicious; they appeared that way as an effect from the higher proof alcohol he'd been drinking.

He spotted the broken DVD player on the floor.

"Not serious, huh?"

Peter stumbled to where the DVD player lay on the floor and hunkered down, nearly falling over in the process.

"It's just the little tray you put the disc in, Dad. We can probably fix it ourselves."

"You know who's good at this sort of thing?" mumble-asked Peter.

Hilary and Adrienne, who'd been stifling their disgust at the musty, sweet odor of their father's breath as soon as he came near, were snapped out of their revulsion at the question. They knew exactly who he was alluding to when he asked it.

That spoiled nerd-slash-brat Arnie Sedgwick.

Hilary jumped into the conversation fray instantly.

"Dad, it's fine. We…"

She couldn't finish her sentence, however, as her father stood up, swaying a bit.

"Arnie can fix it for you guys. Kid's all about his electronics and his games. Little weird shit."

Peter awkwardly made his way back up to the first floor of their house, presumably to call the Sedgwicks.

Adrienne and Hilary waited until he closed the door to express their extreme disapproval.

"Fuck," said Adrienne.

"Kids' so fucking weird, why is he coming here?"

"Because Dad thinks he can…"

"Adrienne. He comes here all the time. Why does it keep happening?"

Adrienne considered the question for a moment, and two answers sprung to mind.

"Could be for a couple of reasons."

"What reasons," asked an increasingly annoyed Hilary.

"Maybe it's Mrs. Sedgwick's way of rubbing what happened to mom in our faces."

That explanation pissed off Hilary further. Saying it out loud only saddened Adrienne.

At that moment, the lights in the basement flickered on and off several times. A strange noise, or more accurately, strange noises, echoed through the room.

The sound of a howler monkey screeching off in the distance. Rhythmic chanting during a ritual. A torrential downpour upon an infinite number of trees.

The mysterious sound and light show ceased within seconds, however.

Despite the brevity of the phenomenon, the Newcomb sisters were completely freaked out.

"Was that… a jungle I just heard?" asked Hilary.

"I can't tell if I'm happy that you heard it too or frightened to death that you did. Least I'm not crazy," replied Adrienne.

The two of them sat petrified, in silence for minutes, that felt like hours instead. Hilary regained herself first and returned to the conversation they were having just before their basement went full Paranormal Investigators.

"What...what was the other reason?" Hilary asked.

Adrienne was still stunned.

"Huh?" she replied.

"What was the other reason why Arnie keeps coming over here you said?"

Adrienne shook her head, clearing it.

"I thought that maybe Mrs. Sedgwick…"

S E V E N .

"…feels bad about what happened with their mom, Arnie," replied his father.

Arnie looked at him and flashed a 'you can't possibly be serious' expression. To his credit, his father responded with 'I had to say that' look.

There was no way in hell Susan Sedgwick ever felt badly about anything.

The SUV that Arnie and his father took to make the drive over to Newcomb's house pulled onto the bridge that connected the waterfront neighborhoods of Arcadia Bay to the rest of the town. When the vehicle had traversed a bit more than halfway across, both Arnie and his father were assaulted by the distinct, pungent, and seemingly ubiquitous odor that characterized that area of town.

"Ugh Dad,I told you!"

"Ya, I know Arnie. Just roll up your damn window, boy."

Arcadia Bay, as the name suggested, was a coastal town. Among its more unusual characteristics, other than its propensity for sinkholes and earthquakes, was that Arcadia City's coastline was not remotely scenic or picturesque. There was not a beach to be had at any point within city limits, the entire stretch delineated by large, jagged rocks instead. To make matters worse, at the northern end of town, a wastewater treatment plant had been in operation for a good ten years before Arnie was born. In that time, the facility had been quite literally turning the "bay" part of Arcadia Bay into an actual toilet.

Municipal authorities insisted that the waters in Arcadia Bay were safe to swim in, issuing their official statement via the town's website. However, many of the town's residents happened to notice a footnote in a much smaller font at the bottom of the third page of said decree.

Apparently, the town's definition of "safe" had a shelf-life of fifteen minutes of swimming at any one time, and no more than an hour total for a week.

Arcadia Bay had grown so foul with pollution that it became known throughout the entire state as "Diarrhea Bay"

As a result, the neighborhoods built directly on, around, or near that factory of human waste were of a significantly lower socioeconomic level than their counterparts in the more affluent areas of the town. The affluent areas where the Sedgwicks still lived and where the Newcombs used to make their home.

Arnie and his father were only a couple of minutes away from Adrienne and Hilary's house. Since his father had given him a bullshit answer to the question of why it always seemed that his mother wanted him to go hang out with the Newcomb sisters, his mind raced. He hadn't been able to shake what that response implied, despite its obvious falsehood.

Why would his mother feel bad for what happened to Mrs. Newcomb in the first place? It's not like it was his mother's fault that Mrs. Newcomb did what she did.
Or was it?

"Dad, why would Mom feel bad about Mrs. Newcomb anyway? I mean, so she'd always send me over here to hang out with Hilary and Adrienne. I told you before the drive. They don't even like me."

The SUV pulled into the Newcomb's driveway.

His father put the vehicle into park and took a deep breath.

"Son, Mrs. Newcomb had problems. Serious ones, too."

"Like what, Dad?"

His father turned to him.

"Maybe when you're older, Arn. Now go. You keep asking me questions you ain't gonna live long enough to get your answers."

"But…"

"Arnie, fix their DVD player and just hang out for a few hours. Be back at nine."

"Fiiiine," Arnie said and got out of the car.

Carl watched as his son first knocked, then was let in by Pete. Carl waved to Pete, and Pete returned the gesture. That was good — the man wasn't so drunk that he couldn't open the door and at least pretend he wasn't killing himself with booze.
The door closed.
Carl thought about what he'd said about Mrs. Newcomb having 'problems'.

The woman only had one.
She was far too trusting of people.

E I G H T .

The twice-monthly book club Susan invoked as if it were a banishment spell cast upon her husband and son had been a near-religious tradition for the women of Evergreen Estates for several years. The book club had started mere months after the houses of said real estate development had all been occupied, and without fail, it had served as the primary social gathering for those women who belonged to it.

The prices of the homes in Evergreen Estates started at prohibitive amounts when the first properties went on the market. By the time the last houses were up for sale, they'd reached astronomical levels. But despite this aspect of the neighborhood-to-be, every home had been bought up months in advance of the first projected move-in date.

Or maybe it was because of that aspect. Evergreen Estates offered an insulated and therefore removed section of Arcadia Bay that allowed those with the bank account and/or income to never have to look upon, let alone intermingle with the 'common' residents of Arcadia Bay.

These were people that possessed no interest in seeing how the other half lived in any way.

The first book club meeting had been organized by none other than Barbara Newcomb. She'd be struck with the idea over dinner one night, when it had been just her and the girls (Pete was away on a business trip).

Adrienne and Hilary couldn't stop gushing about a young adult adventure series they'd both been reading, Barbara barely getting a word in edgewise as they went back and forth. It dawned on her at that moment how it would be a great idea to get to know the other women, and by proxy their families, if they had a regular meet-up.

A book club was as good as any other excuse to have a small get-together, who really gave a hoot if they spent even a minute talking about some novel only a few of them read anyway.

So Barbara spent the better part of the evenings of the following two weeks going door to door, making full use of her considerable communication and diplomatic skills, and rounding up the womenfolk of Evergreen for the first ever book club.

Barbara's day job was CFO of a highly successful brokerage firm in Los Angeles, so suffice to say her interpersonal skills were of an exceptional level.
One of the women she'd met on those afterwork sojourns through the neighborhood happened to be Susan Sedgwick.

On the evening Barbara first came to knock upon the Sedgwick's front door, Susan answered.

"Uh, can I help you?"

Barbara's usual, practiced corporate cool demeanor and approach vanished in an instant. There was something immediately off about this woman.

Barbara said nothing at first, stunned into silence by the aura of belligerence radiating outward from this woman who stood before her.

"I said…"

Barbara managed to snap out of the spell she'd fallen under. For a moment, she considered saying something like 'sorry, wrong house,' and walking away without mentioning anything about her little tete-a-tete she'd planned.

Her conscience got the better of her, however, and Barbara stayed on mission.

"Hi there! My name is Barbara Newcomb. I live up the street here and to the left, on Denmore Ave."

And then whatever that "off"-ness was that Barbara only sensed at first came straight to the surface.

"Oh! Hello…" Susan had flipped from the outward countenance of menace fueled by a bottomless pit of belligerence to cordial, polite diplomacy in a split second.
The sight of Sedgwick's impossibly fast transformation was one of the most alarming things Barbara had seen in quite some time.

"Well, ah, Mrs. Sedgwick, is it?

"Yup!" her smile grew even wider. Sedgwick looked like a crocodile that had somehow taken human form in every aspect save for its teeth.

"I just wanted to come by and introduce myself, and then invite you along to a get-together I'm hosting. Kinda like a neighborhood women's club if you will."

Susan frowned.

"That sounds like the stupidest thing I've ever heard." Barbara frowned.

And over those same six months and despite that first strained encounter, Barbara and Susan grew to have a working, cordial friendship. At least, that's what Barbara regarded it as.

For Susan, she had simply been keeping her enemy as close as possible.

Susan resented, loathed, and hated Barbara. Her natural beauty, easygoing and laid back charm, and her almost supernatural way of becoming the center of attention in any room she stood in drove Susan absolutely insane.

Susan wanted to be the alpha of the group, the one the rest of the women looked to for how to act, how to dress, and how to carry themselves. Susan was convinced that's the way this little group should have been from the start. Her husband had been in the goddamn NFL, after all.

And then, as if the gods decided to smile upon Susan Sedgwick, Barbara made a terrible mistake.

Barbara confided in Susan.

What had been confided, in hushed speech and in a moment where just the two of them stood together in Susan's kitchen, was the kind of information that could destroy a person's reputation, life, and standing in the neighborhood if handled correctly.

Barbara said:

"Susan, wanna let you in on a little secret. Maybe it could help you and Carl out in the pocketbook."

Susan perked right up.

"Oh? Do tell, my friend," she replied, slithering across the kitchen to stand next to Barbara at the sink.

"There's a company called MetaPod, kind of a start-up in Los Angeles. They're about to drop this interactive gaming thing - it's like an immersive game."

"You mean like, virtual?"

"Yeah, but this is way different. The player hooks in, and it's like they're actually in the game. Smells, sounds, feeling, the whole thing."

"So why…" Barbara grew impatient.

"Because their stock is gonna go through the roof, girl. Me and a couple of others down at the firm got all our war chest tied up with them. Gonna make a killing…" Barbara trailed off at that last, returning to the living room to where the others were laughing and drinking.

Susan merely eyed her rival from the kitchen, smiling. Insider trading.
Gotcha, bitch.

She whispered: "Law of the jungle, cunt. Kill or be killed."

The following day, Susan wasted no time in notifying the appropriate authorities, then, after the news had broken on a few major networks, made the rounds calling all the other book club members to sufficiently disgrace Barbara's good name.

Barbara was arrested that afternoon and bailed out of jail by seven that night.

Barbara had known, the instant the FBI stormed into her office, that Susan had taken the clandestine information she'd imparted to her and used it to destroy her life.

All for a fucking book club.

Barbara and Pete arrived back at their place around nine. She saw a few of their neighbors standing out on their lawns, gawking at them as they arrived.

"I'll never go against my instincts again," she mumbled in a stunned, zombie-like manner.

"We'll get through this hon. Promise," said Peter.

Evergreen Estates was the safest neighborhood in all of Arcadia Bay - in fact, zero crime had occurred in that development since it had opened, if one didn't count Barbara's white-collar crime.

This didn't deter Pete from insisting they keep a handgun in the house 'just in case', and for 'protection'.

Upon entering their house, Barbara walked upstairs to her and Pete's bedroom. She pulled the .38 from underneath the neatly folded sheets in the bottom drawer of their dresser.

She'd known that Pete kept it loaded. She
sat down on the edge of her bed, clicked
the safety on the firearm, and stuck the
barrel of the gun in her mouth.

Barbara pulled the trigger, there was the
loud snap characteristic of a lower caliber
handgun's shot, and blood and brain and
bone rained upon the duvet cover as quickly
and in large quantities as a tropical
rainstorm over the heart of the Amazon.

NINE.

Susan woke up in her bed a few days later,
feeling more refreshed, invigorated, and
energized than she had in years. Her enemy
vanquished, she grabbed her cell from the
nightstand. She logged in on her banking
app and saw that her and Carl's checking
balance had sprouted extra zero on the
right-hand side of the total figure, just
before the decimal point. Susan wasn't an
idiot. She knew Barbara knew her business.
Just because Susan had outed her to the
authorities, it didn't mean Susan wasn't
going to take advantage anyway.

Diverting any kind of suspicion she may
have aroused by doing so was accomplished
simply by making transactions through
Carl's investment broker, and not her own.

Arnie knocked at the door, bleary-eyed and
half-asleep...

"Mom, can we take a ride to the plaza
today? There's a new game I want to get for
my Playstation."

Susan grinned, much like she had on that
day when she had first met Barbara.. Today,
of course, was the launch of the new
MetaPod gaming system. Arnie would be the
first kid in Evergreen Estates to own one.
The Sedgwicks certainly had the money for
it now...and then some.

And buying it had a certain quality of
poetic symmetry to it as well.

"Sure, Arnie. Actually, young man, I think
you deserve a little more than just a game,
don't you think?"

Arnie's eyes lit up.

"I do?! What could be more than just a
game?"

TEN.

It looks like you guys need a new drive
gear for the little door, Adrienne," said
Arnie, speaking into the tiny rectangular
slot that was stuck in the open position.
He spoke with the air of elderly
watchmaker poring over a centuries-old
timepiece.

Which actually was sort of appropriate,
considering that a DVD player in the mid-
21st century was an electronic
anachronism. Here he was, expected to fix
it, because his parents felt bad for these
two girls for some reason.

All Arnie could think about was getting
back into his MetaPod and returning to his
own private jungle adventure.
Fortunately, this thing, this DVD player,
was built like a kid's toy compared to his
MetaPod.

Because of one silly little gear, the door
wouldn't close. Stupid thing. Figures only
poor people would still have one.

Arnie attempted to use both thumbs to
force the door closed, and when it
wouldn't budge, one of his thumbs slipped,
caught the edge of the door, and took a
three-centimeter chunk out of the side of
it.

"Ow, FUCK," he cried in the half-turned
voice of a boy only months into puberty.

His F-bomb came out in three registers at
once, none of them pleasant to hear. The
wound began to bleed immediately. A single
drop of blood fell from his digit into the
same darkness that Arnie had just
attempted to force the DVD tray into. He
failed to notice, nor would he have cared
if he had. He dropped the device onto the
ground, stuck his injured thumb in his
mouth, and spun around in his lotus
position to face the girl sitting on the
couch behind him.

In doing so, Arnie also failed to notice
that behind him, the DVD player had turned
itself on. A moment later, the disc tray
slid back into its slot seemingly of its
own volition.

Broken drive gear notwithstanding.

"Hey Adrienne. Did you hear what I said?"
Arnie was now upset. And when Arnie was
upset, he demanded attention.

Adrienne, for her part, had checked out of
reality the moment Arnie came down the
stairs and Hilary stepped outside to "use
her cell phone", a barely concealed
maneuver to avoid having to even say hi to
their guest.

When Arnie didn't get the response he felt
as though he deserved, nay demanded, he let
out as loud a disgusting sigh as he
possibly could.

Adrienne caught the end of said disgusted
sigh and returned to the here and now.
She'd been thumbing through a paperback to
ensure she'd only have to barely
acknowledge the presence of the entitled
loser attempting to fix their DVD player.

She looked up.

"So can you fix it, Arnie?" she asked,
ensuring that the mocking inflection she
used in uttering his name was enough to
wind him up even further.

"If you had been paying attention, I said
that this piece of garbage needs a new
drive gear. But what it really needs is to
be thrown in a dumpster."

Adrienne wanted to get up and knock his
fucking teeth out at that very moment. She
knew that Arnie wasn't just talking about
the DVD player, but also the people that
relied upon it for some meager form of
entertainment.

"K. Let's go."
"But where the hell are we going?"

Adrienne got up from the couch, setting
aside the book she'd been reading, titled
ChaoS/HeaveN.

She'd read it so many times, the binding
had failed, and the pages were held in
place with scotch tape and paperclips. The
book was long since out of print. It didn't
matter anyway.

Nobody really read anymore, books having
been relegated to the same media no man's
land as the movies the apparently broken
machine on the floor occupied as well.
Rumor had it that the book was filled with
'forbidden knowledge', whatever that was.

The author had died under mysterious
circumstances.

"Yep. Gotta see Howie for your 'drive
gear'. Or whatever. Howie's got
everything. We got that DVD player in
his shop."

Arnie stood up from his makeshift work
area the exact moment Adrienne arose.
He somehow felt powerless with her
standing over him. It was a feeling he
could not abide, even for a moment. He
really hadn't planned on doing
anything else with this piece of junk
from the dark ages, but Adrienne
seemed to know exactly where to get a
replacement part.

"For real? You know where to get a…"
Adrienne glared at him, impatiently.
Her look was so certain that Arnie
lost the will to finish the sentence.

"Yes, Arnold."

Adrienne walked over to the sliding
glass door that separated what passed
for their outdoor patio and their
basement. The patio had decayed to the
point of broken, loosely organized
rocks and the sand upon which they had
originally been laid upon. Adrienne
banged on the glass. Hilary was just
outside, close enough to hear her
sister's percussions.

Hilary moved the earpiece of phone
from the side of her head and mouthed
"What? Fuck off."

Adrienne mouthed "Let's go. NOW."
The word 'now' exaggerated to
accentuate urgency.

Hilary stomped her foot, spoke a few
more words into her phone, and came
inside.

"Where, Adrienne. Where the fuck are
we going. That was Trevor on the
phone."

"Trevor? From that gross Glo-Bowling
Alley?"

"Oh ya. The hot one."

"Trevor sucks, Hilary. We need a…what
do we need again Arnie?"

"A new drive gear. It's the piece that…" But before he could finish his sentence with what a drive gear does in a DVD player, Adrienne filled in the gap for her sister with language she might actually give a shit about.

"It's the piece that fixes our DVD player, Hilary. We need to go to the shop."

Hilary was quick to respond, "So? Why don't you and…"

Adrienne pounced with tiger-like agility upon her sister and pinched her right bicep, inflicting both shock and pain in each measure.

"We need to go to the shop, Hilary."

"Okaaayyyyyy, jeezus," Hilary replied, gingerly rubbing the contused bicep.

Adrienne had effectively communicated that she had no intention of making the walk to the shop with Arnie alone.

"So what's this shop you guys keep talking about?" Arnie asked.

Adrienne and Hilary exchanged a knowing glance.

"It's a conundrum, Arnie," the two sisters spoke, in perfect creepy-twin stereo.

"What? Is it called A Conundrum, or what?" asked a confused Arnie.

"No, dumbass. It's called…"

E L E V E N.

Howie's Everything and More Store was about a fifteen-minute walk north on River Street, the road that more or less ran parallel to Arcadia's "Gross Coast".

It was a walk that Hilary and Adrienne had taken more times than they could count, at least since Mom had passed and they'd been forced to move into the neighborhood.

The cottages that lined River Street on both sides were each in various states of disrepair, ranging from completely abandoned, boarded up, and with no less than four or five windows smashed out with well-placed rocks to ones that despite still having actual residents dwelling within their walls, they nonetheless were in dire, desperate need of re-shingling, paint, stain, or really just any iota of home improvement that could be managed. There were no lawns to be had anywhere – every yard had instead overgrown with either weeds, beach grass, or both. The residents here still used mailboxes, which meant they still relied on snail mail, another dead giveaway of the poor and impoverished in that day and age.

As they walked, they passed more than a few dyads and triads of individuals here and there hanging around seemingly doing nothing but lingering on this corner or hanging around in that yard. Each bore the expression of one that had been brought down to a more savage state not by any overt act, but the quiet yet still quite violent machinations of society writ large. As such, each person, male, female, boy, girl, or any other seemed to have some rudimentary plan of evening the score percolating just behind their eyes.

But regardless of their respective surliness, each group greeted Hilary and Adrienne with a bro-nod of respect, a 'sup', or were out-and-out ignored altogether. Kin recognizes kin, so to speak.

Each group did, however, take notice of the pussy-ass rich kid in their midst, and those percolating plans appeared to hit a boil as Arnie passed each. Adrienne nudged Arnie along whenever he seemed to lag behind, for fear the kid would end up getting the ever-loving shit kicked out of him.

Hilary, secretly hoping that someone would in fact staple Arnie's face to the pavement with their fists, took notice of this phenomenon and wryly remarked: "Welcome to the jungle, Arnie."

Arnie, for the life of him, did not see the environs of Jungle Adventure 3 anywhere, and didn't understand the reference.

"Huh?"

Hilary rolled her eyes."It's a line from an oldies song, Arnie."

"Oh. I don't really like music, Hilary."
"Yeah, right. You play in that MetaPod thing all day long."

"Duh. It's so awesome. I just got this game called Jungle Adventure 3. You guys probably don't know about it. Anyways. With the upgrades my mom got me..." and off Arnie went for the rest of the journey to Howie's. Adrienne and Hilary tuned him out the second he went into detail about those upgrades his mom got him - his new MetaIntutitive Interfaces, his new Real Time EnvironMents; and then kept him that way throughout all of the other nonsense he spouted as they walked.

Adrienne and Hilary were happy nonetheless - they were out of their house, away from their father, and on top of that? They were going to see Howie. Howie was cool.

At last, the front display windows of their retail-oriented destination appeared - a few hundred feet away at the end of the block they walked upon. Howie's occupied the opposite corner at the four-way intersection ahead of them. As they approached and the sundry items in the display windows became visible, Arnie couldn't begin to guess what kind of store this place was even supposed to be categorized as.

"What the hell" was all he could muster for speech, the front glass doors no more than fifty feet away.

"Howie's is a bit of a conundrum for someone like you Arnie. It's got everything," interrupted Hilary, "and nothing."

Hilary loathed the sound of Arnie's voice and she'd had quite enough of it by that stage of the journey. She'd just cut him off and also fucked with him a bit as she did so.

Adrienne, Hilary, and Arnie finally came upon the main glass double doors. Beyond them, there shone a few light bulbs that hung shadeless from the ceiling at irregular intervals, only dimly lighting the area within.

Adrienne turned her attention away from the store and looked back upon the street, it was only then that she seemed to notice that the sun had given way to night completely. She seemed to panic at the thought.

"Hilary, what time is it? Howie might have actually closed up already."

Hilary pulled out her blue Nokia cell.

"Only 7:15, freak. We've got fifteen minutes."

Adrienne turned back from the street towards the store. She looked relieved. Howie kept the place open until 7:30 Monday through Friday so that when he did finish wrapping up his business, it was 8 o' clock and time for Star Trek and Doctor Who reruns. And, as if on a kind of metaphysical cue, Howie himself knocked on the window, smiled, and flashed a 'the hell are you guys doing just standing there' look at them. Hilary opened the door, and the teenagers disappeared into the store. Arnie commented something about how the Book Club meeting must have started by then.

TWELVE.

Back at Arnie's house, the Book Club had never started at all. His father Carl had sent out a group message at 6:55pm to all invited to turn their white asses around, go home, Book Club was canceled. By 7:15 pm, he'd wrapped up leaving a voicemail message for a golfing buddy of his, a prominent divorce lawyer.

He'd made his plan to call that friend, the aforementioned divorce lawyer, after learning that his wife of nineteen years was directly responsible for Barbara Newcomb's death.
Carl hadn't known about the encounter Susan had with Barbara in their kitchen.

He hadn't known about the call Susan had made to the feds just hours after that encounter. The call that alerted them to Barbara's illegal, yet nearly impossible to catch, and almost impossible to prove financial activities. He hadn't known that the windfall that they'd come into while all that ugliness went down was made possible by the very same information that Barbara had given Susan.

Lastly: He hadn't known, truly known for sure, that his wife was capable of such savagery. There'd been hints, of course, here and there over the years. But these hints had only been that. Hints. Eyebrow lifters. Head scratchers.

What Susan had perpetrated upon the Newcomb family, and the benefit she'd reaped from the human misery she'd sown in that poor family were not the actions of a civilized human being. Forget civilized, even. Forget human.

These were the deeds of a sentient reptile.

It had started with a question, innocent enough for starters, but one Carl felt he'd never been given the true answer for. Susan was never one for overt gestures of sympathy (which made far more sense in the current context), yet whenever that stupid Book Club of hers had their little get-togethers, she'd never once failed to send their son to the Newcomb's.

Revisiting this weird tradition of his spouse's was foremost on his mind when he returned home from driving Arnie.

Carl marched straight to their kitchen where Susan was finishing her prep for her guests with the slicing up of thousands of dollars of exotic meats and cheeses.

Carl came right up behind Susan, deftly grabbed the kitchen knife out of her hand, and then tossed it aside.

"Why the Newcombs, Susan. Every time you have these assholes over to compare bank accounts and toys and fake tits, you send me over to drop our son with that poor family."

Susan turned around, alarmed but only for a moment. Her face then morphed into a façade of cheerful repose.

"Carl, honey, I've told you a million…"

"BULLSHIT, WOMAN," he erupted. "What game you think you're playin' with me?"

Susan sighed and stepped around her husband.

"Guess we're going to do this now. Fine."

When she spun around to face her husband, a man over a foot taller than she, the look upon her face was that of a practiced serial killer. The ex-NFL player stepped back in reflexive fear. His balls retreated into his body like frightened snails.

"Barbara Newcomb told me all about MetaPod's stock the night before she was arrested."

Carl was no genius, but he wasn't stupid either.

The statement Sue had just uttered made it immediately clear that Sue had been the source the Feds had to bust Barbara.

"You..."

"Shut up, Carl. Don't say a fucking thing until I'm done." Susan paused and took a deep breath.

"Patriots, pound sign, the number 2, the number 7."

Carl's jaw dropped to the floor. It was his password to his secret pension account. He'd kept it up to have a source of income unknown to Susan in case of divorce.

"Why would you do that, Sue. How could you possibly hate somebody that much to ruin their life like that?"

"Because nobody is better than me, Carl. Not her, and not you. For years and years, it's always been Carl Sedgwick and family. The big NFL player and his forgettable little wife and kid." Sue took a giant gulp of overpriced wine.

"Fuck that. And fuck Barbara Newcomb. I've been playing second fiddle to her cracker ass since we moved into this suburban nightmare. Now I run that stupid club and decide who's what and when. I'm the chief of this tribe, and I decide who gets fucked and who thrives. Me." Sue smiled, triumphantly.

Carl Sedgwick had gone toe-to-toe with football players three times the size of a normal human and had never felt afraid of even one of those gladiators. He was stone petrified in the presence of the person-beneath-the-mask that was his wife.

"Are…are you going to do anything to me, dear?"

Sue took in her husband's fearful countenance and met it with sheer mockery and laughter.

"Oh, honey," she said, pursing her bottom lip in a pantomimed sad-face. She approached her husband and caressed his cheek.

"You can be so cute sometimes. But stupid, though. I already did what I wanted to do to you. I cut your balls off when you weren't even looking."

'What?" Carl asked.

In an instant, Susan flipped to sheer rage.

"THE MONEY FROM YOUR PENSION, SHIT FOR BRAINS! It's YOUR money I used to make millions, and its YOU that'll fry if you even think of going Boy Scout on me. And on top of that?"

Susan leaned in and whispered into her husband's ear.

"I'm the provider in this house, Carl. Not you. Think we'd still be able to afford this place, this neighborhood, on your retirement alone? Not a chance, asshole."

Susan turned and walked away from her husband, towards the stairs to their bedroom. She stopped short and turned back to Carl.

"I sent our spoiled, perverted little son over to the Newcombs every Book Club night so I can tell all these cunts that show up I do that, so it seems like I have such a big heart, and that I'm still such a good friend to Barbara, even though she's gone. Every single one of them eats it up."

"You're a monster, Susan."

"Of your own making, number fifty-six."

"I was fifty-three, Susan."

Susan turned around again and made her way up the stairs. She called down to Carl when she reached the top.

"I don't fucking care, Carl."

After finishing with his golf buddy turned divorce attorney, Carl made his way downstairs and stopped by the living room where Susan relaxed with another glass of expensive wine and the book that was to have been discussed that evening. She took notice of her husband's presence after a couple of minutes.

"You know, nobody even reads these things anyway. Who even reads books still?"

"I'm going to get our son."

"I don't fucking care, Carl."

"And then we're leaving. You'll hear from my-"

"I said, Idon'tfuckingcare."

THIRTEEN.

Hank Murray heard the jingling of the bells above the entrance doors to Howie's. A fresh wave of panic swept over him.

Up until the moment he detected that sound, he'd been the only one in the store over two hours before it had been made.

He'd been frozen-in-place, unable to move. Not even a pinky.

The place in which he had been rooted to had been a spot about halfway down the final aisle, at the rear of Howie's.

In those two hours, Hank had also pissed his pants, twice even, out of sheer fright.

Just a few feet away from him, there stood the apparition of Barbara Newcomb. This apparition was nothing like any ghost should look like.

It just looked like Barbara had, with only one major exception. Her jaw was mangled, hanging from just one corner at the side of her face like a broken bloody hinge. Her tongue resembled a fleshy firework that had exploded early down her blouse. There was not a tooth to be found in the menagerie. From the phantasmagoric menagerie of her face, there were streaks of blackened flesh within the area that had been her mouth, gunpowder burns and scorches from when Barbara had shot herself.

Despite this facial carnage, Hank could hear the disembodied voice of Barbara in his head as clearly as if it had spoken aloud by an intact jaw, mouth, and tongue.

"Here he comes, Hank. Remember what you promised me."

"The Sedgwick kid. Give him the DVD," he replied, except he did so with thought instead of speaking. In his left hand, there appeared a small plastic case, his fingers just slightly enough to hold the mysterious movie firmly in his palm.

"Wha...what movie is it Barbara?" thought-asked Hank.

He looked directly into the hideousness that shone in the ghoul form of Barbara, and within that countenance, Hank could have sworn he could see a kind of foul, full-toothed smile within.

"It's called Cannibal Apocalypse 2, Hank," whispered the demon.

Hank nearly dropped the second he heard the title.

"So you've heard of it, then, Hank?"

Again, Hank felt the presence of that awful, ethereal smile.

"You…you can't," from Hank's mind.

The Barbara-demon flew at Hank, stopping just an inch from his face.

He could smell her putrescence emanate from the bodily chaos of the ghoul's neck, face, and jaw.

"CAN'T I...HANK? LITTLE ARNIE WANTS AN ADVENTURE,AND HIS CUNT MOTHER WANTS TO BE THE CHIEF OF THE TRIBE. I'M ONLY GIVING THEM
WHAT
THEY
WAAAAAAAAANNNNNNNT."

At that instant, every part of Hank's body released from its supernatural hold. Freed from invisible prison, he first instinct opened his mouth to release the loudest terror yell he could achieve. Hank sucked in a massive amount of air to blow it out.

And then, there came from behind him the voice of a teenage boy.

"Mr. Murray? You uh, you okay?"

Hank stifled the eminent scream that had fully formed but hadn't been released from his lungs and throat. It had to go somewhere, however, before he uttered a word to the kid, which most definitely was Carl Sedgwick's perverted little offspring. In a flash of inspiration, he thought to push the excess air out of his lungs slowly, through pursed lips, as if he were blowing out a birthday cake.

"Hey, Arnie. Fine. What are you doing?"

"Mr. Murray, I can't hear a thing; your back is turned."

Hank considered this. Arnie was looking right at him, yet wasn't completely terrified as he did so, which meant...

Hank looked ahead of him, to the end of the aisle. There was no sign of Barbara-ghoul anywhere. He relaxed his shoulders and then, faced the boy with as forced of an 'everything's cool' face as he'd ever made in his life. While he did all this, Hank ensured he held the DVD case in such a way so that Arnie could see the cover art and the title. He held it thin-side straight down, with the flat side outwards. With his strings automatically pulled by anything associated with a jungle or something with a jungle directly printed or visible on it, Arnie's eyes zeroed in on the DVD the same way a predator does when it catches sight of its prey.

"What's that, Mr. Murray?"

"Oh this?" Hank held it up to the kid so he could clearly see the title as well.

"It's one of those things called DVDs. They were like-"

"Movies, yeah, I know."

The kids' eyes had gone from bleary, mostly closed and half-asleep to those of an addict upon seeing a half-ounce of blow once he'd caught sight of that DVD, just because it had a couple of fucking trees on it.

That ghoul had known that the Sedgwick kid was going to react like that. For a moment, Hank considered pulling it away from the kid, doing the heroic thing.

And then he remembered what Barbara promised would happen to him if he failed to get Arnie to take the DVD. Hank handed it right over the second the kid reached for it. He'd decided that having "his right arm torn from its socket and stuffed up his ass, while the left would be forced down his throat, so he could shake his own fucking hands in his stomach," as the ghoul had previously ensured.

Adrienne and Hilary had been going back and forth with Howie about whatever a "drive gear" was the entire time. They'd been at it for so long, that the subject was only starting to come to a resolution as Hank and Arnie emerged from the back of the store.

"Girls, I'll say it again. Drive gears don't break. They're just little plastic wheels that sit on a little metal pin inside the deck."

Hilary, sadly born without the faculty of patience, was ready to punch Howie despite the man's previously established, overall coolness.

"Well then why did Arnie say-"

"Why did Arnie say what?" he asked, appearing behind the girls at the counter.

"That the gear-thing-whatever was broken. We needed to come down and get a new one," said Adrienne.

Arnie stepped forward and addressed Howie, who was also now without patience.

"Uh Howie, sir?"

"Yeaaah?" muttered the overweight and irritated store owner.

"I know that the DVD tray rolls in and out on that gear. The door wouldn't go in, so it had to be it, right?"

Howie's brow furrowed into a furry grey 'U' shape. What the kid said didn't make any sense. The gear was seated on a single pin, which meant it rotated freely. So?

Howie stopped this train of thought before it ran off the tracks. He sat up, breathing loudly as he did. He turned around to the counter behind him, where another of the ancient devices sat. He slammed his fist down on it, scaring his four customers for a brief moment.

The tray slid out from its slot slightly, and Howie yanked it out, breaking it as he did. Howie picked out the gear and gave it to Adrienne.

"There. Go nuts kids. I'm closing."

Arnie began to bring forth the DVD that Hank had just handed to him.

"Uh, Howie, I just need to pay for this."

"Don't worry about kid, just hit the bricks. All of yas."

Adrienne, Hilary, Arnie, and Hank stepped outside.

"You kids need a ride home? I'm going that way. Get you home faster."

Get Arnie to play that stupid DVD faster is what he meant to say.

"Uh, sure Hank," replied Adrienne.

As they loaded into his vehicle, Adrienne, who'd caught a distinct acidic, acrid odor coming from Hank, happened to glance around his pant legs.

This man had recently pissed his pants.

But by that point, it was too late to refuse his offer of a ride home.

F O U R T E E N .

The Sedgwick house was silent.

The meticulous home décor of each ground floor room told silent stories of expensive furnishings purchased at stores mostly unheard of, complimented with various antiques procured by professional buyers on behalf of the Sedgwicks - and not the Sedgwicks themselves.

And all of these things were the trappings of an affluent family and one that made sure that others knew exactly how affluent.

Nobody to know how affluent the Sedgwicks were on that night, however. All rooms were empty.

Susan was upstairs, laying in the bed she and Carl had shared for nineteen plus years of marriage. Five of those years had been truly blissful. They were the first five, unsurprisingly.

Love was still a thing she could experience in those days, the future a magical place she and Carl were destined to reach together. Then Arnie came, and these things changed.

It's not worth revisiting, thought Susan, still dressed for the party that never happened. She hadn't even the slightest notion to take it off, nor would she have even if the thought crossed her mind. Since Carl had taken the time to call each and every single person and/or couple just to take their asses home, she decided that she'd have her own party — and remained dressed for the occasion. Carl be damned.

She thought: Motherfucker just had to say it like an asshole. He had to embarrass me.

Susan, however, did not allow Carl's childish gesture to get under her skin. Not. At. All. She supposed it was his idea of exerting power over the situation — a demonstration to both her and everyone in their social circle that her parties only happened because he allowed her to have them. He was still the final word in the Sedgwick household, despite any reports to the contrary.

She grinned up at the ceiling. What he failed to realize was that in making his way through every local number in his cellphone to crudely vocalize his neighborhood-wide directive, he'd broadcasted to their peers that he, and not Susan, was the source of their marital difficulties. Carl came off as an unhinged man with an axe to grind - and a bone to pick with anyone and everyone.

"Fucking idiot," she whispered.

And their son, Arnie? Lately she'd begun to wonder if the kid hadn't developed some kind of weird sexual mental illness with the pod she'd bought him.

Oops, she thought, and smiled again. She didn't care. Susan had determined that Arnie was a terminal-level dunce, just like his father was. Except Arnie inherited too much of her family's physicality, and ended up as smallish, awkward, and lacking in any kind of strength. He was still his father's son. They both got that brain-dead look on their face whenever confronted with anything above seventh-grade mathematics, and after so many years it had grown to be too much to take.

And what about that MetaPod thing, anyway? The kid spent actual days inside of it. What could be so addictive, so alluring about it.

"Fuck it, Susan. Give the thing a try.

You know Barbara would approve!" At that, she cackled.

F I F T E E N .

Susan got up, and casually traipsed to her son's room. Inside, the MetaPod door still lay on the floor next to the pod itself. Fucking Carl. Breaking a twenty-thousand-dollar toy just 'cause he can't handle being told by a woman what to do.

Susan climbed in.

As she completed the minor gymnastics routine to get into the damn thing, her left knee caught an edge of exposed metal. It had been damaged and thus exposed because of Carl's earlier tantrum. The collision between metal and flesh and bone drew a decent gash just below the knee, where it met her tibia.
The pain did not affect her as much as it should.

She'd finished that bottle of wine from earlier, and half of another.

She failed to notice that the small, vaguely round pool of blood that accumulated on the floor of the pod seemed to be drawn into the stainless steel with which the floor had been fashioned. To an observer, it would look like a more brutal take on the absorbance of a new kind of paper towel.

The MetaPod whirred to life when the floor finished its crude vampirism.

"Well, that's weird," mumbled Susan.

She then assumed that was what it was supposed to do. As the first menu appeared and was barely intelligible from the light that streamed in from Arnie's bedroom, she realized she'd forgotten the door.

"FuckingCarl," she grunted, leaning over the side of the machine and pulling the door up and into place. It wasn't difficult then to secure the door to its slots on either side of the entrance to the MetaPod.

Jungle Adventure 3 began and gave her several options of characters to play. She eventually discovered Yanomamo Chieftain, and that appealed to her. The image of the character in front of her looked odd, like it hadn't been part of the original design of the game. Susan knew absolutely nothing of such things, but even she could tell that there was something off about it.
It didn't matter.

Susan Sedgwick had fucked her enemies up, removed them from her way in real life. She was the boss bitch and wouldn't let anyone ever forget that. Made perfect sense to be running the show for a bunch of Amazonian tribesmen.

She smiled at the thought of the tribesmen, and thought that if her warped-ass son could get some simulated action, she could too.

Susan affixed the VR goggles and started her game.

Adrienne, Hilary, and Arnie jumped out of the backseat of Hank's sedan the second it came to a stop, possibly even before it actually had done so.

Hank had been freaking them all out for the duration of the ride back to the Newcomb's.

It wasn't really what he'd been doing during the ride that was so alarming, although his open-wide, frantic, nervous eyes darting in every direction was difficult to abide.

The three of them, Arnie, Hilary, and Adrienne entered the house and went in three different directions.

Adrienne went to check on her father.

Hilary went downstairs and then to her preferred position outside on the patio, safely away from any more Arnie nonsense and nerdery.

Arnie first went to the bathroom, triggered by some smell he'd detected inside Hank's car. After he'd finished, he went immediately downstairs to start his repair of the DVD player.

He was positively ecstatic now to do so, now that he had an adequate substitute for his MetaPod game.

He came upon the DVD player and looked down at it. It was then that he noticed that the tray door was closed. He pushed the "open" button. The loading tray slid out, completely functional.

Arnie was confused but didn't dwell upon the inconsistency. He decided at that moment he'd tell Adrienne and Hilary that he'd fixed it.

Arnie popped open the DVD case and was immediately angered and aggravated. It wasn't the actual movie Cannibal Apocalypse 2.

All the disc had written upon were two words:

DVD Extras.

"Goddamnit," he said... Arnie put the disc inside the player, and stood back from the television to be able to see what those extras actually were.

From directly behind him, no more than a few inches, a woman laughed maniacally directly into his ear. He spun around, his eyes wider and whiter than dinner plates, his breath frozen dead in his lungs.

The basement was gone, nowhere to be found.
Arnie Sedgwick found himself surrounded by the endless emerald of the Amazonian jungle.

S I X T E E N .

Adrienne had just finished tucking her father, who'd passed out cold before they returned from their excursion, into bed when she heard banging at their front door.

She went to answer it, totally unsure of who was there.
When she opened it, she was surprised to see Arnie's father standing there. Those 'Book Club' popularity contests the adults in her old neighborhood continued to have usually lasted well past midnight.

Arnie was sent over "to fix the DVD player", but everyone concerned knew it was to ditch the kid at their place for the night. It was only 8:30, and here Mr. Sedgwick was to get Arnie.

"Uh, Mr. Sedgwick, come in."

The look on the man's face alarmed her. She'd never seen this man look anything remotely shaken, or rattled, even scared. At the moment, he looked as if he were all three at once.

"Thanks, Adrienne. Need to take Arnie with me early tonight. Some stuff came up."

"Is everything okay?"

Carl looked at the teenaged girl standing before him and felt a great swell of guilt, remorse, and sadness. Could he tell her the truth? If he did, would it have mattered?

"Uh, yeah. Just need to get him early. You don't mind, do you?" Carl knew the girls couldn't stand Arnie. Hell, even he had his moments. Earlier today, when he caught him bashing his bishop in his little freak pod was one.

"Come on in. He's downstairs, watching some weird jungle horror movie he found down at Howie's earlier."

The guilt, sorrow, and remorse vanished instantly. Terror replaced all three.

"What did you say?"

"A jungle... horror... thing... movie.
DVD. Said he found it in the back of
the store when we drove home with that
guy Hank who lives next door to you."

"What in the hell was Hank doing
there?"

Adrienne shrugged.

Carl pushed past her to the basement
staircase. Adrienne followed just
behind as both descended to the
television room at the bottom of the
stairs.

Arnie was nowhere to be found. The
movie played on the television, but
both failed to notice, at least at
first, the action on the screen.

Carl turned to Adrienne, who had only a
look of unknowing on her face. She
grasped for, and found the only answer
she could have mustered at that moment.

"Maybe he's outside with Hillary?"

Carl moved quickly to the glass slider,
and yanked it open, almost breaking
that door off its hinges the same way
he'd broken the MetaPod door off its
own.

Hilary was standing outside, talking to
Trevor again, when she heard the slider
door hit its stop with a sharp bang.
Frightened, she spun around to see the
imposing figure of Arnie's dad standing
there. The man looked frantic, and
terrified.

"Hilary! Where's Arnie?!"
"What? He's inside watching some
weird…"
"HE'S NOT INSIDE HILARY! WHERE IS MY
SON?"

There was a second of silence. And
then, from behind Carl, came first a
shriek, and then a sobbing. It was
Adrienne.

Weakly, her voice could be heard from
within the basement.

"Mr. Sedgwick? I found Arnie."

Carl spun around to see Adrienne
pointing at the television. The man
drew in closer to it, unable to process
what his eyes told him.

Maybe if he looked closely, it would be just a
trick, a vision brought into being by his
emotional state.

It was not a trick.

Carl's lips trembled. His hands began to shake.
He looked down at the ground, catching a glimpse
of the cover of the DVD that Arnie took from the
trip to Howie's. Printed on the cover was the
title of the movie:

"Cannibal Apocalypse 2"

Drawn upon that plastic slipcover in red
lipstick - therefore not part of the original
packaging and a clear message to those who would
be watching the movie next, were two more words:

"Barbara's Revenge"

Carl looked back to the television, and watched
as his son Arnie, frightened to the point of
open crying, wailing, and calling for his
mother, fumbled his way through the thick,
impossibly green overgrowth of the Amazonian
jungle.

After a minute of taking in his son's anguish,
Carl Sedgwick, a man who'd struck fear in the
hearts of professional quarterbacks as a career,
cried out.

"AAAAAAAARNIEEEEEEEEEEE!"

Arnie knew the second the Newcomb's basement
vanished and the jungle around him appeared,
that the place in which he found himself was no
simulation, no Jungle Adventure 3, no MetaPod-
sterilized version of a jungle.

There was no sweetness of smell, only rot,
corruption, and oily smoke from a nearby fire.

An insect larger than Arnie's foot, black,
yellow, and gray with a seemingly infinite
number of legs began to work its way up the
boy's inner calf muscle. Arnie cried out in
disgust, his voice reverting from his recently
achieved, slightly deeper tone back to a pre-
pubescent and therefore higher pitch. The shriek
was indistinguishable from a girls', and loud
enough to alert the occupants of the fire that
Arnie had smelled.

He heard footsteps, branches snapping, and
shouting in a language he couldn't parse.

54

There were natives approaching from all directions. At least, it seemed that way to Arnie.

He panicked and bolted in the direction of the clearest line-of-sight. An absolute mistake, as the clearest line-of-sight also meant the boy was painfully easy for the Yanomamo, the largest and most dangerous tribes in this fictional version of the Amazon, to track and ultimately run down.

Arnie made it fifty feet from his starting point before he found himself stumbling past a large e. A slate gray rock, held in the hand of one Yanomamo hiding behind that same tree, swung into his forehead and made direct contact. The rock broke the skin, peeling off a two-inch square flap of skin and fracturing his skull at the point of contact. The blow also caused a fine mist of crimson to erupt from the wound, as if a spray bottle of blood had been squirted instead of Windex or similar cleaner.

Arnie fell to the ground, unconscious.

It was then that Carl had the thought to send the girls upstairs before it got any worse. He'd heard of Mondo movies before. Never saw one. Knew what happened in them. It was never anything short of obscene and grotesque.

This thought was followed by another, more promising one.

Shut the damn thing off, Carl.

He cursed himself silently for not thinking of it earlier. Didn't matter. He had to try now. His guilt at not killing the power to this electronic video prison that his son had been trapped in did not last long.
Despite all his attempts, Carl couldn't shut off either the television or the DVD player. The on/off switches on both devices were useless.

Predictably, yanking their power cords out of the walls failed to have any effect. Carl went so far as to first wrap his hand in a towel, and then throw his hardest right hook square into the television screen. He nearly broke his hand in the process. After pulling his hand back, shock waves of pain from the impact his fist made on the magical, unbreakable cathode ray tube, he glanced over to Hilary who was sat on the couch behind him. She was staring at the DVD cover.

She looked up at Carl.

"Why does it say Barbara's Revenge on it, Mr. Sedgwick?"

There was no lying, no delaying the answer any longer.

"Arnie's mother killed your mom, Hilary," he monotoned.

"What?" Hilary mumbled.

Adrienne, who stood by the slider door, reflexively punched the glass upon hearing the truth come from Carl's lips.

"I fucking knew it."

And then, in an almost breathless whisper, Hilary uttered one word, intonated as a question rather than a statement.

"Mom?"

The shot was a medium one, from a short distance. The villagers continued their transport of an unconscious Arnie through an overgrown patch of jungle. And just to the right, much closer to the camera, stood Barbara Newcomb, waving. She was physically intact, with no head wounds to speak of. She wore a pristine white dress.

She mouthed the words "I love you," and then vanished, an apparition that once gone, left no trace that it had ever been there.

Roughly ten minutes in real-world time passed from when Arnie caught a rock directly to his forehead. By then, his father had taken up a standing position just a couple of feet from the television screen. He stood there, nearly motionless, between Adrienne and Hilary, flanking him on either side. Each had a massive arm draped around their shoulders.

Neither Carl nor Adrienne nor Hilary realized how tightly the three of them held each other, but even if they were able to, what they watched on the screen would likely cause them to huddle together even more closely together, should that had even been possible.

Arnie had just been brought into the central area of the Yanomamo village, stripped naked, and left in the dirt while twenty or so Yanomamo danced around him. At some point, he must have regained consciousness from the head wound he'd sustained. The injury was growing more and more serious as it continued to hemorrhage down his face. By the time the Yanomamo began their ritual movements around his flailing body, his entire face had been colored a glossy kind of crimson color.

The film continued.I t had been shot on exceedingly poor stock – the imaging was blurred, and its flimsy production material would occasionally make popping noises from time to time.

Additionally, the found footage-style camera work was disorienting at best, motion-sickness-inducing at worst.

The shots constantly spun, shifted, and darted back and forth from one camera position to another. Arnie could be seen for a split second, followed by several more shots of aggressive villagers chanting, then shots of the village, and finally back to Arnie for another split second or two. Each time it did, it became clearer and clearer that the boy had begun to experience severe brain damage.

It worsened quickly.

At the last in this series of shots, Arnie had been rendered incapable of human speech. What had started with cries for his mother, ended with garbled, incoherent not-words and grunts.

All at once, the tribesmen stopped their dance. The camera centered on a hut nearby and zoomed in on a darkened door.

From that darkness emerged Susan Sedgwick, bearing just enough resemblance to that woman as to be recognized by Carl, Adrienne, and Hilary. Her dark skin had been painted with a kind of white and grayish resin, rendering her eyes as nothing more than holes. This was frightening enough to behold, but as she came into full view, and her ceremonial garb became visible, it was abundantly clear what the worst aspect of her appearance bore the worst threat.

She had been fitted with a kind of rudimentary harness, and the harness had been fitted with a thickened length of wood, vaguely straight, two feet in length, with jagged, cruel points at one end consisting of thick, splintered segments of rock and splinter...
But this was merely the garb, elements of ceremony.

Susan's face had been altered so dramatically that she bore no resemblance to the carefully. Pieces of bone, wood, and steel had been pierced into cheek, lip, chin, eye, ear, and forehead.
White paint had covered her face in reversed blackface.

The white present in her eyes seemed to glow in contrast to her makeup.

She strode over to the circle of tribesmen. Most of them began to dance again, but two of them took Arnie by his arms, and forced him face down into the ground. One of them pulled his legs up, such that his knees were bent and his posterior tilted upwards.

From somewhere nearby, but still out of sight, came the laughter of the architect of this ritual. The ghoul watched as her betrayer and the woman who'd orchestrated her downfall unknowingly was about to sodomize her own son to death.

Barbara Newcomb brought her hands to her mouth in pure glee as it began to unfold in front of her.

Susan came up behind Arnie, and once in position, guided the sharpened point into the tight orifice of Arnie's anus. Once it had found purchase, Susan began her thrusts.

Five and the wooden, jagged stick had entered the boy's anus to about five inches. She howled in triumph, louder and louder until reaching a crescendo at the fifth.

Blood ran down Arnie's legs to either side, a wellspring. Occasionally, the camera caught tiny bits of feces being carried out of his body by the currents of red that streamed down.

Arnie could only emit a weak, staccato grunt as each motion back and forth penetrated further and further.

The scene lasted close to seven minutes, and by the time Susan withdrew the ceremonial, yet cruel phallus from her son's asshole for the final time, it had reached a depth of sixteen inches.
The stick was slick and black with all of the bodily fluids that Arnie's flesh had shed upon it.

Arnie was still alive when the two tribesmen that held him in place released him.

One of them produced a sharpened rock hammer and struck at the boy's neck until he had been decapitated.

The entire tribe stopped as Susan reached into the bloody, tangled mess where the head had been attached. She reached into the hole, and found a dollar sized chunk of skin and muscle. She ripped it from that hole, pulled it to her mouth, and greedily began to devour it.

The rest of the tribe then began to tear the boy's corpse apart, feasting upon what was left of Arnie Sedgwick.

The girls wept, falling to their knees.

Carl turned around and dry heaved three times...

There was nothing in his stomach. He composed himself.

He walked up the stairs and back outside.

Once out in the street, he called the police.

A short time after that wild ceremony (what a rush!) and without warning, the MetaPod went entirely dark.

Probably having a bit too much fun, thought Susan. There had to be some kind of restrictions on the content of these simulated games and that's what shut it down, she told herself.

She fumbled around in the darkness. At once, she put her hands into something wet, warm, and sticky. Gooey, even.

"What…" she whispered, and gagged.

The excessive quantity of expensive wine she'd drank that evening came percolating all the way up to and into her mouth, to reach its zenith as a single trickle of red that escaped from her lips. There, Susan steeled her guts and swallowed it all back down into her belly.

To an observer, that trickle would appear nothing like the start of a person getting sick.

Instead, it would be like Susan had just taken a bite of a rare steak. In the darkness of the encapsulation, however, Susan could not see herself.

"How do I get out of this…" she whispered.

And for just a single moment, the MetaPod turned back on – but it only showed a single, frozen image, and only two words could be heard.

Barbara Newcomb. Splayed out. On her bed, in the moment after her suicide.

"YOU DON'T." Barbara's voice. Darkness again.

This was followed by several loud bangs on the MetaPod door.

"Step out of the fucking machine, lady. Hands where we can fucking see them!!!"

"I'm sorry?" Susan answered.

The already broken door seemed to fly off its precarious perch in its closed position. The light from her son's bedroom flooded the interior.

Rather than acknowledging the three sidearms that were pointed at her head as soon as the door came off, Susan took in what was strewn about the MetaPod she'd bought for Arnie.

The remains of whom were now littered and painted on the floor, walls, and ceiling of the device.
Here were the entrails upon which she'd greedily taken simulated bites from. There were the genitalia she'd ordered torn from Arnie's crotch.

He'd only just started growing his first pubic hairs, that would never reach full length or amount. She looked down to her lap, where the decapitated head of Arnie sat, mouth agape, eyes slack in their sockets.

She began: "I don't fucking c…"

All three sidearms rang out, as the police that brandished them decided wordlessly and unanimously that there would be no arrests that evening.

Susan did not finish, but her last word ironically would have been 'care'.

CloSing CrediTs

This Has Been DOUBLE FEATURE: MONDO APOCALYPTO!
"Gary Spivey (Has Foreseen This)" & "DVD Extras"

w/ short films "Amanda" & "Tomorrow"

WP Quigley would like to thank the entire staff of DOUBLE FEATURE magazine for their love & support in getting this thing off the ground: Rich Wiley, Ed Ryan, Eric Blackwell, and David Hannigan for staying as brothers, Theresia and Matt Canniff, Jaime Smyth, Karli Tobias, Erica Johannesen & Rick Walsh, Felicite Valentine, Mom, CLR, and any/all of those brave souls that have stuck around through this year.

Chris Philbrook would like to thank the entire #ringfamily for their ongoing support.

Melody Alice would like to thank Lucienne LeBeau and WP Quigley for their gracious invitation to contribute to DOUBLE FEATURE. She would also like to thank her partner for supplying her with endless cups of hot tea, and who never says no when she asks to adopt another cat.

Lucienne LeBeau would like to thank everyone at Double Feature for their hard work, and WP Quigley for his willingness to share his brainchild.

Michael Strong would like to thank everyone on the team for their efforts, and Nix Black for making the art look easy, because we know it's not.

Nix Black would like to thank WP Quigley for believing in them like an absolute madman, Rich Wiley for introducing us, and everyone else at Double Feature/Ascendent Publishing for being such an amazing and talented crew, and for assuring them that they can, in fact, do the things, and Mom, E for cheering me on, K, and of course, Morla and Viago. ✕

Fin.